FOR ALL TIME

BY

RHEA SILVA

ALSO BY RHEA SILVA
TAMING MARIA
RITE OF PASSAGE
THE DARKEST MASTER

If you want to be on our confidential mailing list for our Readers' Club
Magazine (with extracts from past and forthcoming titles) write to:

CONVECTO READER SERVICES

Box 101
City Business Centre
Station Rise
York
YO1 6HT
United Kingdom

Telephone: 01904 525729
Fax: 01904 522338

NEW AUTHORS WELCOME

Please send submissions to
Convecto Communications
Box 101
City Business Centre
Station Rise
York
YO1 6HT

Silver Moon is an imprint of the Convecto Media Group
First published 2009 Convecto
ISBN 9781-904706-81-Y
© 2009 Rhea Silva

PRELUDE

Smoke rose straight as a poker, casting shadows on the altar. It seemed to the young man kneeling before it that the deity moved: an almost life-sized figure, awesome in its barbaric power, with a bearded face, a head sprouting horns and a bare, muscular torso. The hips and hairy legs were that of a goat with an enormous, erect phallus. The great god Pan in all his glory promised wealth and fertility.

'Give me what I pray for,' the man begged. 'I have my title, this house and estate, a lineage that goes back generations, but I need the insurance that this will continue. I want to devote my life to pleasure. You have heeded me ever since I discovered this shrine. In return, I have given you virgins' blood. Many a girl has surrendered her maidenhead to me, not only for my satisfaction, but as a gift to you. Tonight will be no exception.'

It seemed that the god smiled sardonically, and he thought he heard him whisper, 'You're a devout worshipper, Lord Sebastian. I enjoy the little blossoms you ravish, and marvel at their simplicity. They believe it when you say that you love them and will make them mistress of Daubeney Manor.'

Sebastian felt no qualm of conscience. He admitted that he was totally selfish and used everyone for his own gain, avid in the pursuit of pleasure, exploring unusual byways and draining sensuality to the dregs. He was proud of his reputation as one of the most dissolute rakes in the whole of eighteenth century London. Handsome, charismatic, there was no shortage of women, or men, eager to accept his invitations to riotous orgies held in his magnificent grounds.

He had inherited shortly after returning from the Grand Tour of Europe, an educational trip to which every youth of substance was despatched. Impressed by the Palladian architecture of Italy, he had built a mock-ruined folly. When digging out a grotto beneath it he had chanced upon this hidden site. Keeping its existence to himself, he had studied the rare and valuable books on mythology that graced the shelves in his library and became certain that the god was Pan, and the temple constructed by a Roman general after the occupation of Britain There was evidence many years later, that the manor had been built on the site of a villa.

Hungry for knowledge, Sebastian could have been a star pupil at university had this not coincided with his lust for sexual gratification. Never one for the teachings of the Christian Church, pagan gods and goddesses were much more to his taste, and he guarded this shrine jealously, restoring it without aid, wanting no one else to be aware of its existence. Even at moments like this, when his cronies were in the adjoining grotto indulging in an access of wine and fornication, he was making obeisance to Pan.

He unfastened his breeches and released his penis, rubbing it until it started to swell. He continued to masturbate, recalling how Pan was reputed to have taught the young shepherds to do the same as they tended their flocks in the Grecian landscape. He watched his appendage grow, stretching the foreskin back from the shiny red helm, a drop of dew hanging from its single eye. The sight enflamed him and he could feel the need to spurt becoming more and more urgent. He delicately

4

smoothed the fluid over the end and pleasure coursed through him. He stopped just in time, allowing the fire to die down. He must save it for the virgin who awaited him.

Still exposed, he pushed aside the crimson velvet curtain that draped the entrance and let himself through the cleverly concealed door and into the passage beyond. The voices became louder, laughter and shouts rising above the sound of violin and harpsichord. Sebastian unlocked another door and paused, a cynical smile lifting his lips as he perused the scene. A dozen or so men and woman in all stages of undress sat or sprawled on couches, though some staggered about the finely appointed cave that lay beneath the folly.

The walls were draped in red and black, and hung with paintings of rural scenes where bacchante and satyrs romped in the woods, each graphic in its representation of carnality. It was a perfect venue for wild parties, and Sebastian had taken full advantage of it.

And there was the hapless virgin with whom he could do as he willed.

She stood between two hefty guards, a slender figure in white, head lowered, her long blonde hair falling across her breasts. The rowdy group became silent as Sebastian approached her. He reached out and placed a finger under her chin, raising her face to his.

'My lord.' Her expression was one of relief, her wide blue eyes filled with adoration.

'Bethan. How lovely you are.' His voice was deep, caressing, and she swayed towards him.

'You do me too much honour, sir. I can hardly believe that you have chosen me, out of all the ladies you could have asked to be your wife.'

The hush was almost tangible, then a peal of raucous laughter broke out as he said, 'You are right to think that, my dear. Did you really believe that a chambermaid could become Lady Bartram?'

'But you said … promised … that if I came here tonight, you would announce our betrothal.'

'She is absolutely delightful, Sebastian,' one rakish fop exclaimed, running a hand over her curves. 'Such sport, my friend. May we all have a poke at her, once you've done the de-flowering?'

'You may, Rodger. I shall have finished with her then.'

Rodger laughed. 'You will have done all the hard work, leaving her nicely moistened. Maybe even eager for more.'

She shrank back but was restrained by the hefty henchmen. 'My lord, if you don't want me, then let me go!'

'Too late, sweetheart. Your reputation is already tarnished. You must do as I say if you wish to remain in service here, or else you'll be turned out with no reference and nowhere to live.' He jerked his head towards the guards. 'Strip her!'

She shrieked as they seized her flimsy garment and tore it off. Crouching, she tried to cover her breasts with one hand and her pubis with the other. The debauched crowd gathered round like hounds at the kill, and she was lifted and fastened face-down to a cross-piece, arms outstretched and wrists fettered by manacles attached to chains. Her legs were tethered and a spreader inserted at the ankles, keeping them apart. She was helpless and sobbing and Sebastian rejoiced at the sight.

His cronies were egging him on, bucks from town who shared his love of gambling, be it on horses, cards,

.anything on which they could bet, including cock-fighting and laying their money on the outcome of boxing matches. Sebastian owned a black slave who he had trained to be a prize-fighter, paying the man a pittance from the large sums he won for his owner. They were in privileged positions, frequenting the coffee houses and brothels, scions of noble families sowing their wild oats before finding a rich bride and settling down. Spoiled, indulged, always in debt and caring for nothing or nobody, they were Sebastian's companions for the time being, though he knew full well that should his fortunes fail, they would turn their backs on him.

They were accompanied by ladies of ill-repute who were happy to be kept in style, never anticipating marriage. Several catamites were in evidence. They had been brought along by those who preferred their own sex. Some wore female clothing, while other were manly, willing to fuck anyone who would pay generously for their services.

Sebastian's lust was roused to fever-pitch. Not only was Bethan desirable, but she was terrified. He was the centre of attention, ready to flaunt his prowess before an audience when he finally entered her. He fished in the pocket of his velvet jacket and took out a white, lace-edged handkerchief, then passed this to Rodger, along with the garment. He stuck out his right arm imperiously and one of the guards promptly placed a short, multi-tailed whip in his hand. The spectators reacted with hoots and cries and advice as to how to lay it across Bethan.

He nodded, and Rodger swept up her hair and pinned it to the top of her head. Her bare shoulders gleamed like alabaster, and Sebastian almost regretted marring such perfection, though his prick was rock-hard as he visualised doing so. He took up position, booted feet apart, legs spread in the tight fitting breeches, belled sleeves of his pristine shirt caught in at the wrists above a fall of lace, and his member jutting from the opening in his attire. Now was the moment he had been working towards.

He swung up his arm. The flogger hissed as he brought it down across Bethan's shoulders, resounding in unison with her first, agonised shriek. The audience whooped. Sebastian raised his arm again and treated her back to the lash. Bethan jerked against her restraints as it contacted her, leaving a trail of marks on the tender flesh that had never before known violence.

'My lord, have mercy!' she sobbed. 'I love you.'

'That is a foolish thing to do.' The whip struck her buttocks and Sebastian watched the reaction as they turned pink under the onslaught.

It was too much for his control. He flung it aside and ordered her release. She fell into his arms and he carried her to the couch that was positioned centre-stage. He lay her down amongst the silken cushions, aware of the crowd gathering around, but more conscious of her fork surmounted by golden floss, her vulnerability and his prick. He pushed her legs apart and knelt between them, guiding his weapon towards her virgin sex.

She struggled and kicked until two of those closest held her legs, then hoisted them up, one on each of Sebastian's shoulders. A couple of women gripped her arms, and he penetrated her, slowly at first, while she screamed and protested, and then with a hard thrust, burying his length in that untried orifice. She gave up fighting, collapsing like a rag-doll, the tears running back across her temples and into her hair. Sebastian withdrew momentarily, signalling for the handkerchief and then wiping the vaginal opening. Its pristine freshness now bore crimson stains.

Duty done, Sebastian abandoned himself to completing Bethan's violation. Propped on both taut arms, he drove his weapon into her with brute force while she writhed and cried out. Within half a dozen strokes, he reached his apogee, semen pumping from him to fill her channel. She lay still and silent, while he withdrew. He fastened his breeches and a servant helped him into his jacket,

'Can we use her now?' Roger's eyes shone with eagerness, his cock already at full stand.

'Do what you like?' Sebastian had lost interest.

He left them to it and went back the way he had come. The candles were burning down in front of Pan, and he imagined that the god was smiling in anticipation. Sebastian placed the blood-stained handkerchief before him and bowed, before returning to the ravished girl and his hedonistic companions.

Chapter 1

There was a message on the Internet. 'Couldn't get through. Ring me. Urgent. Andrew.'

'Up yours!' Freya muttered, pressing Exit. 'Goddamn men. They all want to boss you around.'

'Surely not *all*.' Joan looked across at her, smiling, new to the combat zone and still retaining illusions.

'The majority, given half a chance.' Freya was in a bad mood, caused by another of that alien breed, her boyfriend, Carl, or rather her ex. They had been arguing all weekend and this had resulted in her kicking him out. No wonder she hadn't answered Andrew's calls.

The first thing she had seen on booting up the computer in her office, was his peremptory message. 'Bad timing,' she thought, but picked up the phone.

He answered straight away. 'Chalmers here. Oh, it's you, Freya. Where the hell were you? I've been trying to get hold of you since Friday.'

'I *am* permitted time off,' she reminded frostily, swivelling her operator's chair from side to side as she pictured him — longish brown hair, thin face, hazel eyes, an athletic frame. He was quite something.

'I know all that,' he snapped. 'But this is important.'

'What is?'

'I'll tell you if you give me a chance.'

'Calm down. Who has rattled your cage?' Although he was the head of department, this never stopped her talking straight.

'I want to get on with this new assignment. It sounds just up your street. You must have heard of Daubeney Manor?'

'Of course.' It was almost an insult to infer that she hadn't. There were no ancient buildings in the area that were unfamiliar to her.

'Well, we've got the chance to investigate it.' He brought this out as if he was offering her a treat which, in effect, he was. There was nothing she enjoyed more, apart from sex, than rooting around a site that reeked of history. Daubeney was one. British Heritage had been dying to let loose their experts on it.

'How so?'

'Come to my office and I'll explain.'

'OK. Be there in five.' She replaced the receiver in its cradle and turned to her colleague. 'Hold the fort for me, will you? Got to see Andrew.'

'Right you are.' Joan saluted smartly and went back to her screen, then added, 'Don't do him under the desk.'

'Would I?'

'Yes, especially if you've just had a spat with Carl.'

Did it show that much? Freya picked up her bag and notebook and paused in front of the mirror, deciding that she looked positively haggard. She regretted coming in that morning, could have rung with some excuse about a cold or headache. My God, she mourned. There's no disguising my age. Every year of twenty-five and then some. What is it some clever person once said? "Love is a universal migraine." That's it. No more romantic attachments for me. I'll stick to bricks and mortar.

The face staring back at her was pale with dark smudges under the eyes, surrounded by layered and high-lighted hair. She was a touch too thin, often forgetting to eat properly when caught up in an absorbing project. She remembered that she hadn't stopped for breakfast, eager to get out of the place that had once been a love-nest but had turned into a cage.

Would Carl come back? Probably not this time. Their affair had run its course and he was a player. She couldn't trust him and didn't intend to share him with half a dozen others. She was worth more than that.

She squared her narrow shoulders, straightened her spine and lifted her breasts, muttering, 'Tits to Jesus,' as she had learned during flamenco classes in Spain, then marched out of her office and headed along the passage towards Andrew's. A tap on his door and she was inside. He was standing by the window of the modern block, staring across the river below.

'Freya.' He turned and came towards her, hands outstretched.

The touch of his firm, warm fingers was momentarily comforting. Here was a man who made no secret of his admiration. She had warded him off, remaining faithful to Carl, a quite ridiculous situation considering how he had been spreading it around. Never could keep it in his trousers.

'Sorry, Andrew. I was busy all weekend.' To her horror she found that she wanted to cry.

'What's wrong? Carl been acting up?' It was impossible to pull the wool over Andrew's eyes. He didn't miss a trick.

She took a chair on the opposite side of his desk, as far away from him as possible, afraid that she'd crumble like custard if he touched her again or subjected her to his concerned gaze. Only then could she trust herself to answer. 'We've had a row. It doesn't matter. Tell me about this new job.'

He picked up a biro and spread out papers. 'I thought

it would be just up your street. We've been wanting to get our hands on Daubeney Manor for yonks, but it's been empty. Now it has recently been sold to a writer named Maxwell Sinclair.'

'The authority on temples and old religions?'

'That's him.' Andrew steepled his fingertips together and regarded her over them. 'He's put in a planning application to extend, so we finally get to look over it.'

Although in the usual way Freya would have been raring to go, now her attention wandered and she mused on the possibility of ignoring Joan's warning, diving under the desk, unzipping Andrew's pants and giving him a blow job. He shot her a sharp stare, almost as if he could read her mind. Had she been young and green, she might have blushed, but as it was, she said, steadily, 'That sounds intriguing.'

'I thought you'd think so.'

'When do we start?'

'There are a few formalities to go through. He has already moved in. I'd like you to phone him and arrange a date for a visit.'

Mr Sinclair doesn't stand a hope in hell of preventing examination of the property, she decided inwardly, having seen Andrew in action before, a force to be reckoned with in the board room. Argumentative committees and county councillors collapsed under the blast of his dedicated determination that not a single stone of a building that he had taken under his wing should be disturbed without permission.

She reached across, saying, 'May I see?'

He pushed over a plan of the property and its surroundings. Her attention was immediately captured, all other considerations laid aside. She couldn't remember a time when she wasn't fascinated by old houses and history. It probably sprang from when she was a little girl and her father, a rock musician with a mop of hair and love of composing and playing, would bundle her into his car when he wasn't on tour, and take her out 'looking for ruins.' She had studied architecture at university and, on graduating, had applied for a post in the West of England, settling in the market town of Blackheath, where she had bought a house. Her father was dead and her mother, long divorced from him, had run off to America with the drummer from his band. Freya had no siblings and was virtually alone.

Daubeney Manor. She stared at the photographs and felt it to be familiar. But then, she often experienced this feeling when perusing documents. The pictures and diagrams showed it to be medieval with later additions. There was a lodge, towers and a walled-in courtyard, arrow slits and walkways, a rabbit warren of rooms, cellars and dungeons, all manner of delights to lift the heart of an historian

'Well?'

She came to herself and found that Andrew was watching her. He had the kindest eyes, and they almost put her off the matter in hand. She got a grip and answered, 'Great. I've been dying to see this place.'

'We must make sure that his proposals don't damage too much of the historic fabric. Meanwhile, why don't you let me take you out to dinner tonight?'

This came as no surprise. Whereas before she had fobbed him off if their association had threatened to become something more than businesslike, now her anger against Carl made her think, to hell with him! And she smiled at Andrew and said, 'I'd love to.'

He shot her a quizzical glance. 'My, my, Carl certainly has upset your apple-cart, hasn't he? I should thank him for it.'

Freya didn't move as he stood up and walked over to her, stopping by her chair. She could smell him, a combination of fresh linen, warm flesh, body lotion and that indefinable something that the male seems to exude from his skin. He touched her forehead gently, and she leaned into him.

'Steady, girl,' she warned herself.

The room was isolated. No one was likely to interrupt them, but she was scared of jumping from the frying-pan into the fire. In her experience men were not to be trusted She still yearned for Carl's arms around her, his lips on hers. Yet it was true that he no longer kissed her as he had done at the start of their affair, was more inclined to go straight for the kill, shooting his load, then rolling over and going to sleep. Andrew offered the hope of more.

He cradled her. She felt the hardness of his chest muscles under the white shirt, the slimness of his waist, the press of that as yet unexplored object that firmed out his crotch. It was too soon, and she knew it, placing her two hands against him, putting space between them He let her go and stood back. 'I'll pick you around seven-thirty. We can talk more about Daubeney Manor.'

By five-thirty Freya was walking from her work to home, stopping at the supermarket on the way, to grab bread and a carton of milk. It was strange to become a singleton again, no longer catering for a partner, a state that she hadn't occupied for two years and one she didn't much relish. As she meandered towards the check-out, she struggled to lift her thoughts from the

15

black pit into which they were heading, and console herself with the idea of no cooking for Carl, or washing his socks or ironing his shirts. Surely there were advantages in living alone? She'd been happy enough with it before he blundered into her life and took over.

This proved little consolation as she stood in the queue with other women who might have been wives and mothers, or simply career-oriented like herself. She peered into their trolleys, searching the contents for a clue as to which group they belonged.

How sad is that? she thought, dreading opening her front door and stepping into emptiness.

It happened, of course, and was every bit as bad as she had imagined. She didn't even have a cat to wind round her legs and bully her into opening a tin of the much advertised Kitty-Joy. She smiled wryly. Had it been labelled Pussy-Joy, she might have thought it to be a lubricant.

There was a message on the answer-phone. 'Carl here. I shall be in this evening to fetch the rest of my gear.'

Her heart couldn't have sunk any lower, already lying bleeding over the hall-tiles. 'Sod!' She said aloud, despairing and furious at the same time. 'He'd better leave the fucking key! There's no way he's going to walk in and out of my house as if he owns it!'

The pain was so bad that it forced tears to her eyes. There was no one to see and she sobbed uncontrollably, and then caught sight of herself in the gilt-framed mirror. 'God, what a mess!' She moaned. 'Blotchy, puffy-eyed. Why can't I cry gracefully like Joan who simply sniffles a bit and dabs at her face with a tissue, instead of the bath-towel I need to staunch the flow?'

She told herself to shut up. She was going out with

Andrew in an hour or so. Time to repair the damage. She put her shopping away in the kitchen and went upstairs. This wasn't a picturesque cottage set in an Olde Worlde garden, but one in a row of terrace houses near the brewery, once occupied by labourers. It had been modernised and had two bedrooms and an attic studio. There was a bathroom en suite, a shower downstairs, and a small, walled-in plot of land at the back where she could have grown vegetables if she so desired. She didn't, turning it into a patio for sun bathing, adorned with terracotta pots of flowers. It was hers; no mortgage, bought with some of the money that her rock-star father had left her. She never failed to bless him for this, grieving for him and knowing that she would give it all up for one more hour in his company.

Dashing the tears away with the back of her hand, she walked into her bedroom. Its sash windows over-looked the paved terrace. She noted that the pots needed fresh soil and bedding plants. It was March and more frosts unlikely. Time to think about spring. Normally, she liked refurbishing the hanging baskets ready for lazy days in the sun, followed by convivial evenings sharing the hot tub with friends. But now these simple amusements would pale without Carl.

Had they been happy times? 'No,' she answered truthfully. There was always the maggot wriggling away there, spoiling everything, born of his unfaithfulness and her insecurity. She closed her eyes, blotting out the innocent scene, remembering other occasions. The rows, the accusations.

'I saw you kissing her!'

'My God, you've a fertile imagination. I was doing no such thing!'

'Liar!'

'Jealous bitch!'

'I was humiliated in front of all our friends!'

Tears, denials, recriminations. And she knew all along that she was right, relying on that gut instinct that warns a woman when she is being betrayed. Freya left the window with its too vivid memories and went into the bathroom. A twirl of the tap and the Victorian style, cast-iron tub set on claw feet, started to fill, perfumed steam rising. She undressed in the bedroom and, naked, viewed herself critically. Not bad. Though an erratic visitor to the gym, her body was naturally shapely, her busy lifestyle keeping it in trim. Her mother had been a beauty queen, winning many a contest and her preoccupation with exercise and massage and dieting had put Freya off, but she had inherited her figure.

And much good has it done me, she brooded, as she added another slosh of toning lotion to the water and tested the temperature. Fuck all.

After pinning up her hair, she lowered herself in, relaxing and switching on the jets. Bubbles rose, impudent fingers tickling her sensitive spots, seeking out her erogenous zones. Impossible not to recall hours spent in the bath with Carl, especially in the early days. He would sit behind her while she slid between his legs, feeling his cock and balls against her buttocks. His hands would explore her breasts and mound, slipping into her crack and finding her clitoris, the soapy water forming slippery moisture, adding to that already seeping from her.

You don't need him, she reminded herself sharply. You've always been able to come off on your own. A finger-fuck and, if you want something bigger inside, a vibrator.

Resting her head back against the edge of the tub, she opened her legs wide, feeling the wavelets caressing her folds. She braced a foot on the rim, spreading her labia, exposing the hard nubbin between and training the spray on it. It was a soft, warm, gentle movement, sufficient to send spirals of pleasure coursing through that easily aroused organ, making it swell. This was the position that gave her the greatest sensation, parting her wings with one hand and massaging her clit with the other. The spray was simply an adjunct. She could pleasure herself anywhere at any time and did so frequently, whether or no she was in a relationship.

All thought of Carl vanished. She concentrated on bringing about her climax. Leaving one hand on her clitoris, she moved the other to her breasts, going from nipple to nipple, pinching them into needy points. She palpated her organ, faster and faster, only aware of reaching the peak. The excitement mounted and she was up among the stars, crying out as she exploded, orgasm rippling through her.

She killed the spray and brought her legs together, the water rocking around her as she sighed and allowed herself to rest, part floating. Then, as her heart beat slowed and a sense of well-being pervaded her, she realised the time and hurriedly left the tub.

Back in the bedroom, she riffled through the wardrobe. Usually she was so sure of herself that suitable gear for an evening presented no problem. But this was different. She may have been with Andrew at business functions, but never gone on a date with him. It was slightly intimidating, though she lectured herself while searching. What was she expecting? That he'd want to throw her on her back and shag her? Is that what she hoped for?

19

She hauled out a plain black number, deceptively simple but it had cost. It was superbly cut, with shoe-strings straps and a floating skirt. After laying it across the bed, she got out the body-lotion and rubbed it into her skin. She had always looked after herself, using moisturiser daily, and adding sun-screen when she worked on her tan, liking to look bronzed. Now, after following the skin beautifying ritual, she slipped into a black bra and matching thong. Hold-up stockings with lacy tops came next and she stepped into high-heeled shoes

The dress slithered over her and she adjusted the straps, and added a chunky necklace. Seated on the dressing-table stool, she raked through her cosmetics, cleansing her face and beginning the build-up — foundation, a touch of blusher, shaping her brows, adding more mascara and eye-shadow than usual. Her hair had recently been styled by Dave, who was a friend as well as the owner of a flourishing salon. As camp as Christmas and unfairly handsome considering he was on the wrong bus, he always did her proud. She needed to do no more than shake out the superb cut and run her fingers through it. With a final glance in the mirror, she went downstairs.

The sitting-room was quite plain and ordinary-looking, with little to distinguish it, but there was time for a cigarette and a large G&T. Freya had twenty minutes to spare and contemplated switching on the TV. As it was, she was going to miss her favourite programmes but, soaps being what they were, she'd catch up easily tomorrow. The central heating had kicked in, but even so she was cold and shrugged an exotic pashmina around her bare shoulders. The shock of Carl's abrupt departure had not yet worn off, or the reality sunk in. She poured another gin, downing it in one when Andrew knocked at the door.

The Sambourne Hotel was posh. There was no denying this, but. Freya wasn't fazed by it.

As she said to Andrew when a waiter showed them to a table. ' Posh hotels were a part of my upbringing. Dad took me to stay in them sometimes during his tours.' It was the gin talking. She had not discussed her past much with him.

The waiter pulled out her chair and handed her a menu. Andrew consulted the wine list. 'Ah, yes,' he answered calmly. 'He was Ray Mullin, the rock singer. I always liked his stuff. It was innovative, not the usual run.'

Her hackles went up. Was he being patronising? She wished she'd stopped at one drink. 'He was great.' She was aware that she sounded defensive. 'Mum left and I went to boarding school, but it was OK, an arty-farty, free kind of gaff where most people in the entertainment game sent their children. Holidays I spent with him or with his mother, my gran, who lived with her toy-boy and liked smoking pot. He was killed in a car crash soon after I started at uni.'

'I'm sorry. Remember reading about it in the paper.'

'It was a long time ago now.' I mustn't cry, she thought. Bloody gin! Mother's ruin. But she accepted another while they discussed the menu.

The dining-room was very grand. This had once been a house belonging to a Northern industrialist who had decided to retire to the West Country and chosen Blackheath. Solidly built in the Gothic style so popular in the late nineteenth century, it had all the grandiose features of that prosperous age, chandeliers, oak panelling, copies of Pre-Raphaelite paintings, William

Morris wallpaper. The drapes were sumptuous, the carpets thick, the service impeccable.

'This isn't your first visit.' She relished the exquisitely prepared food and wondered if the chef was one of those television gurus, doyens of the kitchen, who monopolised the screen these days, flirting and flaunting and making the average cook feel totally inadequate. She always reached for the OFF button, but there was no denying the excellence of this cuisine.

'I eat out sometimes and like to try various venues.' He topped up her wine-glass.

She raised it to her lips and asked, 'Alone?'

'Often.'

'Why is that? You're handsome, intelligent, and knowledgeable. What is it?'

He didn't reply until the waiter had finished taking their plates away and fetching the next course. 'I was married — once, and only for a short while. It didn't work out and I've not tried again.'

'You're a bit like me, then. I've had a couple of partners, but have come to the conclusion that I'm better off alone.' Filled with alcoholic savoir-faire, she was finding it easy to talk to this personable man, wishing that she was seated next to him and not on the opposite side of the table.

They were in an alcove, partially screened from the other diners, all well-dressed and well-mannered people. 'Bet they've never known hardship.' She waxed philosophical, then giggled and added, 'But then, neither have I. Dad smoothed my path, and never told me if he struggled to do it. I was cocooned in a cosy world, apart from when my mother left, but I never saw much of her anyway, and Dad was more concerned about the loss of the drummer.'

'You seem competent and able to take care of yourself,' he observed, sampling the pudding that had just arrived.

'It's an act.' She sank a spoon into the confection, mixing strawberry meringue with whipped cream. 'The only thing I'm sure about is my work.'

'At which you're very good. This reminds me, we were going to talk more about Daubeney Manor. I've been on the blower to Sinclair myself, and he expects you at eleven tomorrow morning.'

She felt an unusual rush of nerves. 'Will you come, too?'

He cocked an eyebrow at her. 'Surely you don't need a chaperone, do you?'

'Certainly not.' She pulled herself together, but was disappointed.

'You'll cope fine, though I think you could do with an early night.'

'Do I look that bushed?'

'You look beautiful, as always,' he answered, with old-world gallantry. 'Let's have coffee and then get going.'

Wasn't he about to try it on? She wondered, feeling rejected

Even in the privacy of his car he made no move to snog her and when he pulled up outside her house, it was she who invited him in.' Come and have a drink.'

'I'm driving,' he reminded, but got out and locked the car.

'Well, another coffee then.' She fumbled for her key and, once inside, switched on the light and stood looking up at him, then led the way into the sitting-room, unsure how to handle this situation. Did he fancy her or not? Had she misread the signals?

She was rather disappointed Carl wasn't there. He

was supposed to be fetching his belongings and she had hoped to show him that it hadn't taken her long to find another fuck-friend. He had departed before she arrived, but had left a muddle in his wake and a note that said, 'Shall come with a van for the larger stuff.'

She sighed and turned to Andrew. 'I hope this doesn't descend into petty arguments about who owns the TV or stereo or bed or wardrobe. Thank God we haven't a dog, or that might be chopped in half.'

'Children would be worse. Break-ups are horrible, aren't they? Has it really happened this time? Are you through with him?'

The strong hotel coffee was clearing her head and she began to regret her rash invitation, finding that she wanted to pour out the whole story to him. Excusing herself momentarily, she went into the kitchen, boiled the kettle, got out the Instant and returned with two mugs on a tray. Andrew was looking through her CD and DVD collection.

'I didn't know you liked classical music,' he said.

She put the tray on the low table. 'Oh, yes. Just because my father was a rock-and-roller doesn't mean that he didn't appreciate other forms. I took after him.'

'Opera and ballet? You surprise me. I enjoy them, too. Let's go together sometime. Is Carl a fan?'

'Oh, no. We differed there, as in so many things.'

'You're sorry to see him go, though?'

'You can't live with someone for several years without missing them.'

'Tell me about it.'

Freya selected a recording of a Tchaikovsky symphony, put it on, and then sank into the Chesterfield beside him, glad to have someone to share both the music and the settee.

She lit up a cigarette. 'I smoke, you know, so feel free to do so.'

'I'm trying to give them up.' He took one from his pack.

'Aren't we all?'

They puffed in companionable silence, absorbing the Russian composer's sweeping music. The mock-fire in its cast iron stove sent out flickering flames. The wall lights cast a subdued glow. It was warm, comfortable and secure, and Freya felt happier that she had done for hours. OK, so more positive women like her cynical bosom pal, Moira, would tell her off for being needy, but she couldn't deny that Andrew's presence made all the difference.

She snuggled closer to him and he kissed her gently on the lips, but then said, 'I should be going.'

'Why?' She was disappointed and surprised. 'You can stay if you like.'

He drew back, smiling at her. 'The last thing I want to do is jump you when you're on the rebound. I respect you too much for that.'

'But…'

'No buts. I'd rather take this slowly. I don't think I could cope if you suddenly decided to have Carl back after all.' He was standing now, and she rose and joined him, feeling flat as a pancake.

'I shan't.'

'You might.' He walked towards the hall and she dragged behind him, any confidence that she might have acquired wilting like a water-starved flower.

'OK. I'll be at the manor at eleven, as arranged.'

'We'll meet in the afternoon and you can tell me all

about it' He paused before stepping out into the chilly night, then drew her to him and kissed her again, properly this time, not tongues, but with passion.

With this she had to be content, for the time being, watching his car lights disappearing down the street.

CHAPTER 2

The lodge appeared to be empty. It stood beside the massive, rusted iron gates and a high stone wall that seemed to go on for ever. There was a notice saying, 'TRESPASSERS WILL BE PROSECUTED'

The whole scene had a lonely aspect.

'Charming,' Freya muttered, as she got out of her car. 'No sign of a welcoming committee.'

Her watch gave her ten-forty-five. The appointment with Maxwell Sinclair was at eleven. She hated being late and always gave herself time to spare. She rapped on the door of the quaint little house that should have been the home of the gate-keeper. It was hard to tell if it was inhabited. There were lace curtains at the windows, but no smoke curled from the chimney and it was silent as the grave.

Freya had a reputation for having nerves of steel. She had spent a lot of time alone, rummaging about in cellars, attics and reputedly haunted rooms without freaking out. If there were ghosts, she hadn't been aware of them, yet this deserted lodge sent a chill down her spine. Then she heard footsteps inside and the door opened.

'What is it?' demanded the youth framed there. No phantom. He was very much alive, wearing jeans and a T-shirt. His hair was in a pony-tail. Though he had rings in his ears, he wasn't one of those crop-headed, tattooed louts trying to look as threatening as possible.

'Mr Sinclair is expecting me.' She assumed her most friendly tone. 'Are you in charge?'

'Mum is.' He grinned as he eyed her up and down. No doubt she'd be providing a wank-fantasy later. 'I suppose you want me to open the gates?'

'Got it in one. I'm Miss Mullin.' She held out her hand and he took it. His palm was dry and warm.

'Nice to meet you, miss. My name's Danny.'

'Will you let me in, Danny?'

'OK.' He closed the door, and she heard him in conversation with someone inside. A female. The mother of this prime example of adolescent manhood? Freya decided he was quite sweet

She waited, turning last night's events over in her mind. Her head ached, reminding her that she had drunk too much. She wished she had been able to ring Moira and get her opinion, but she was in Bermuda, sunbathing and screwing her latest conquest, who was the son of one of her best friends.

As she had said when Freya remonstrated about his age, 'Well, darling, were he mine, I'd be grateful to the more mature woman who introduced him to the joys of sex. No likelihood of an unwanted pregnancy or some nasty disease with a long name and unpleasant results, and I've taught him about the clitoris.'

There was no answer to that.

She'd certainly fancy Danny. But I want her here now! Freya raged. I'm in a muddle and my head is fucked. She may be a rat-bag, but she's worldly, knows her way around, a journalist of repute and very little gets her down.

Leaning back against her car bonnet, she waited for the Parting of the Waters, in this case, the opening of the gates. At last she caught a glimpse of Danny on the other side of these wrought-iron barriers. They yielded with surprisingly little effort. 'I've given 'em a good oiling and told the boss-man that he should get 'em fixed so they open electronically. He said he will, when the historic

28

people have given permission. Is that you, miss? You don't look like a boring old fart of a history person.'

God bless him, she thought, confidence restored, though that's precisely what I am, a boring old fart. 'I've come to get a sus on it. Have you been here long?'

'About a month, Mum worked for him in London, but he's left the house there, though it's still staffed so he can go back when he likes. Mum's been organizing cleaners and a cook and whatnot. It's huge, man! Like something out of a horror movie. But we've got this lodge to ourselves and Mum's OK with it. Her boyfriend is the butler, so that's cool. They're getting married soon.'

He seemed to think a great deal of his mother 'What's her name?' she asked.

'Jennie … Mrs Barker.'

'Are you at college?' He was the type who would benefit from higher education.

'Nope. Taking a sabbatical. Getting my band together.'

'You sing?'

'And play lead guitar. The lads come down from London for sessions.'

'You like it here?'

'It's cool.'

She got back into the car and drove past him, waving goodbye as she proceeded along the tree-lined drive. Someone had been hard at it, and the gravel was immaculate, the borders neat and the bushes controlled. The way twisted and turned and she gasped as the manor came into view. The photographs hadn't done it justice. Daubeney was perhaps the most splendid example of early architecture with Jacobean additions that she had yet come across.

It was partially walled-in and must have had a complete

moat at some stage. What was left formed a long pond. She could see two towers behind it. There had once been a hefty wooden gate keeping out unwanted visitors, but this stood wide and she drove into a courtyard, complete with a gatehouse and detached kitchen where the lord's garrison had cooked. There were stone steps leading to a walkway on the outer wall, complete with slits where marksmen could have fired arrows or lead-shot on enemies below, though this might be a sham, a previous owner's fancy.

Freya left the car and stood, scrutinizing the house. It seemed rooted there, as if it had grown organically from the ground, rather than being built by man in the thirteenth century, although subject to changes and additions. She could see that larger windows had been inserted where once the original court-facing frontage would have had few, making it impenetrable to unwelcome visitors. The door was at the head of a flight of wide stone steps, and made of solid oak, the planks placed vertically and crossways, a double skein and very stout. An arch was an addition of around the same period as the wings that jutted on either side. She walked up and hammered on the solid brass knocker.

The pause that followed gave her further opportunity to examine the exterior of this fascinating building. She couldn't wait to get inside. But it seemed that she must, for there was no answer and she knocked again, loudly and persistently.

'All right! All right! I'm coming!' Someone shouted and the door swung inwards, revealing a slim, immaculately attired individual. He was small-boned and pretty rather than handsome.

Freya said, 'I've come to see Mr Sinclair. Miss Mullin.'

'Hello. We're expecting you. I'm Hilary Carr, Maxwell's aide. Come in.'

She stepped into a vestibule and followed Hilary round a carved screen, finding herself in the finest example of a Great Hall that she had ever come across. This would have originally been the centre of activity, used for feasting and family gatherings. Also a place where the feudal lord held sessions in his position as magistrate for the district, settling disputes and handing out sentences to wrong-doers. Hilary dithered in front of her, pointing out this feature and that, as proud as if it belonged to him.

She nodded, drawing her own conclusions, guessing that although the panelled walls were now dark brown, at one time they would have been in much brighter colours. It was the Victorians who had spread doom and gloom. Pausing by the monumentally large fireplace whose hood soared towards the rafters, she absorbed every detail, particularly the crest carved into the stone. It depicted two ravens, with a Latin tag held between their talons.

'The crest of the Norman knight who was given this land for services rendered to William the Conqueror, and built his fortified home here,' put in Hilary, and she wondered how he had managed to soak up so much history in such a short time. Presumably he had arrived with his boss who, according to Danny, had settled there a month ago.

It all seemed a bit too pat; the kind of story anyone would assume to be linked with a French robber baron. She needed to check the archives. The Hall was furnished with a long trestle table in the centre and benches each side, chairs with upholstered seats and heavily carved

31

arms, a pair of great oaken coffers, statues of mythological subjects and landscapes in ornate gilded frames. There were several arched doorways leading off. Flags and pennants, pikes and crossed swords adorned the walls, reminders of battles long ago, and the central staircase was very grand, with carved balustrades.

'Was all this here when Mr Sinclair bought it? If so, how come it hasn't been vandalized while standing unoccupied?'

'The previous owner kept a close eye on it and appointed a caretaker.' Hilary's know-it-all attitude was beginning to get on her nerves.

'It's nearly eleven.' She cut the conversation. 'Is Mr Sinclair about?'

'Certainly, Miss Mullin. Please come this way.'

He walked towards one of the doors and knocked softly. It was immediately opened by a woman in a tailored jacket and skirt. 'Ah.' She held out her hand. 'Miss Mullin?'

'That's right. I'm from British Heritage.' Freya wondered briefly if her designer denim jeans and suede waistcoat were too casual.

'I'm so pleased to meet you. Do come in. My name is Donna...Donna Steadman. I'm Mr Sinclair's secretary. Won't you sit down? Would you like a coffee?' She turned to Hilary. 'Please tell him that she is here.' He looked rather put out, but took himself off.

Freya started to relax. This was a friendly atmosphere and Donna a pleasant, thirty-something woman who indicated a tray that held all the makings, and proceeded to fill two cups, and pass the sugar bowl and cream-jug. She was easy to talk to, keeping up a flow of light conversation mostly concerned with moving to the country and settling in the manor. She spoke very highly of Sinclair. In fact, Freya came to the conclusion that she had the hots for him.

'Is your husband here?' She pushed the boundaries a trifle.

Donna gave a tight laugh, 'Oh, I'm not married. I have far too much to do for Mr Sinclair.'

'I'll bet you have,' Freya thought sardonically. Aloud, she said, 'I, too, am single. My work takes up all my time.'

Liar, she scolded herself inwardly. It's because you've never found a man who comes up to your expectations. You've been through therapy and learned that if you're disappointed it's your business, not the other person's. Disappointment is of your own making. But knowing this and putting it into practice are two entirely different things. Maybe I'll have to go back to my shrink. He was a babe and taught me a lot, but unfortunately it didn't stick. I fell apart again when I met Carl.

Donna's head lifted. 'Here he is!' She jumped up and went towards an inner door.

Maxwell Sinclair entered. He was tall and lean and scholarly-looking, with glasses pushed up on his forehead. His hair was dark and curly, and he wore corduroy trousers and a sweater. Though he gave the impression of being an academic, the glance he gave Freya made her feel as if he had penetrated her physically. He had the most extraordinary, golden brown eyes. A phrase came to her unbidden. *Wolf's eyes, gypsy's eyes.*

He took her hand and shook it. 'You are from British Heritage, under Mr Chalmers.' He stated this as a fact, and his voice was deep, cultured and captivating.

She didn't want him to view her as Andrew's dog's-body and answered quickly, 'We are colleagues.'

'Ah, yes. He spoke highly of you. Said you were an expert in early medieval buildings.'

'I have made a study of the subject.'

'Where would you like to start?'

'I want to look over the whole house and perhaps you could tell me what your plans are, then I'll report to Mr Chalmers and his team. We can take it from there.'

'That sounds reasonable.' He accepted the cup of coffee Donna handed him and strolled to the window embrasure, looking out. 'I've made a thorough survey myself.'

'I understand that you are familiar with the subject.' She didn't know what else to say, thrown by this man with the film-star looks, who appeared to be so confident.

He turned with a smile. 'I've spent years studying buildings that hold so many secrets. One never knows what one might unearth.'

'I find that, too,' she put in quickly, scrabbling for common ground. She placed her cup on the table, aware of Donna's needle-sharp eyes.

'You've finished? Then I suggest we take a look around.' He nodded to Donna. 'I'll conduct Miss Mullin myself. There is no need for two of us. Littleton Press is waiting for that call concerning my contract. Will you sort it out?'

Of course she would! She'd wipe his arse for him if he asked, Freya thought pithily. Donna was jealous of her, although keeping up the pretence of sweetness and light, so she added to her chagrin by switching on her most dazzling smile and preceding him through the door, note-book in hand.

Hilary was hovering in the Great Hall, but he was

dismissed and Freya led through the ground floor rooms by the great man himself. 'Call me Maxwell,' he said. 'And yours?'

'Freya.' There was a barely tangible shift in their relationship, but she was well aware of it and so, she imagined, was he. Now he became almost comradely, as if they were sharing an adventure.

'You were named after the goddess of spring.'

'That's true, but one of my friends also christened her wolf-hound that.'

He chuckled and, for the first time, humour lifted his mouth and tiny laughter lines creased the outer corners of his eyes. The sternness vanished and she wanted to take his hand and run through those lofty rooms and up the stairs to the Master Chamber, there to fall into the vast seigniorial bed and make passionate, uncontrolled love.

She dared not look at him, having the uneasy feeling that he guessed what she was thinking. Instead, she concentrated on all he was telling her, having to admit that he knew history inside out. It was impossible to fault him. They passed through corridors linking splendid apartments, up staircases and traversing the Long Gallery where, on wet days, the ladies and children of the family would play carpet bowls or stroll and talk, admiring the latest portraits perhaps. It had been kept in a good state of preservation, though a fortune needed to be spent on re-roofing. Maxwell, apparently, was willing to foot the bill.

'You are lucky to be in the position,' she said, as he pointed out a damp stain running down the side of one of the bedroom windows. She added it to her already copious notes.

'I've worked hard for it.' He sounded angry, as if there was much more behind this, and she didn't pursue the subject.

The attic was a rabbit-warren where once servants would have slept. It was used for storage, and in a dilapidated condition. Maxwell insisted on showing her everything. Where there were no light bulbs, he produced a torch, flashing its beam into cob-webby corners and dim nooks, lifting the lids of travelling trunks to display a wealth of clothing from former days.

'Fine for dressing-up parties,' she observed.

'Very true. But you've come here to see bricks and beams, crumbling chimney-pots and missing tiles, not relics of a family long-gone.'

'I understand there was no one left to inherit. All were dead or hadn't the money for the upkeep. It's the same story all over. It costs too much.' She closed the trunk.

'D'you want to come below? The cellars are interesting.' He assisted her down the steep stairs and they stood on a landing that connected with the kitchens, the servants quarters far removed from the apartments of their lords and masters.

Freya had experienced enough for one day, but there was no way she was going to chicken out. She suspected that he was taking her on this extensive tour deliberately. Hoping to scare her off? She wouldn't put it past him. He was a difficult man to read, too canny by half and his sheer physical attraction was weakening her resolve to stay cool, businesslike and super-efficient.

'It will be necessary for my team to explore any subterranean rooms ...cellars and wine-vaults, dungeons, crypts. It's all part of the survey. I can take a cursory look now, if you wish, then return with reinforcements.

There's much more detail to be had, apart from all you have shown me so far. Photos, measurements, assessments and repairs. It's going to take time.'

He lifted his shoulders in a shrug. 'That's fine. I shall bury myself in my study out of the way. I'm writing another book.'

They descended to the basement .A stone sink and old fashioned dresser stood there, and an antiquated Aga in the hearth where once food had been cooked on an open fire. This was used for the hot water and there was a shabby electric stove.

'I want to modernize, installing a proper central heating system, an up-to-date cooker, a dish-washer and built-in cupboards in here, and a washing machine and dryer in the laundry.'

.'That sounds reasonable, though you'll have to submit plans, '. Freya commented.

He cocked an eyebrow at her. 'I hope they won't take long to go through, or I shall lose my staff. I'll take you to the wine-cellar.'

They had reached a door set in one of the thick, white-washed walls. The air smelled musty. He switched on a light and they went down. 'These weren't here, I take it?' She smiled, staring at the row upon row of wine racks, each holding a bottle.

She knew little about wine, but thought that Maxwell might be something of an expert. He seemed to be that kind of person, but she didn't encourage him by asking. Wine buffs could be a bore. It was cold there, as it should be for storing vintage plonk, she imagined. They walked slowly up and down the aisles.

'I brought the wine from London. One needs a fine vintage. I give dinner parties and entertain sometimes.

My butler is in charge.' He paused to draw out a dark green bottle and study the label.

'Would that be the fiancé of Danny's mother, who lives in the lodge?'

'Yes, that's Armitage. He's been with me years, and she, too. Danny is a bright boy. I hope he was polite.'

'Oh, very. The first person I met here.' Freya was getting cold now and wanted to leave.

She'd seen enough of Maxwell and Daubeney Manor for the time being. It would be pleasant to be in the company of someone straightforward, like Andrew. It wasn't anything she could put her finger on, but Maxwell made her uneasy. He, apparently, had not finished, for now he said, 'We can go further down, to what used to be the dungeons. There's no lighting there, I'm afraid. I'll use a candle, far more atmospheric than a torch.' He led the way.

Freya started to shiver. If it had been cold in the wine-cellar, then it was twice as chilly here. She cursed her pride that simply wouldn't allow her to give up on a project. By now, she could have been warm and dry in her own house, terraced though it was and in no way grand, but more comfortable by far than this dark, dank, rat-hole. The steps were slippery, and there was no hand-rail. Maxwell went first, the candle throwing a yellowish uncertainty on walls where water glistened, punctuated by the iron bars of heavy doors.

'It's no fairy-tale then?' she muttered, edgily. 'This really was a dungeon.'

'Oh, yes.' He lifted the candlestick higher, illumining the dismal scene. 'A prisoner might be locked in here, never to be seen again.'

She couldn't tell if he was serious or just trying to

frighten her. She pulled herself together with an effort. 'I've been in such places before. Most unpleasant. I gather that you are intending to preserve it? I'm sure we shall want you to do so.'

He chuckled. 'No trouble. I'll be able to scare my friends when I throw a party. "Behave, you lot! Or into the dungeon with you!"'

The candle-light threw weird patterns on his face, making it seem harsher, and an answering laugh stuck in Freya's throat. It wasn't funny. Was he joking or would he really do so? By now, she was beginning to think him capable of it, although nothing in his behaviour had been conducive to causing alarm. This was short-lived.

Without warning, the flame was extinguished. She as plunged into inky blackness. 'What's happened?' she cried, expecting him to flick his lighter and touch it to the wick. 'Maxwell! Are you there?'

There was silence. Then she heard him breathing and put out her hands, wanting to feel something human and real and solid in that pitch darkness. Her fingers met empty air. Where was he?

No time had passed since the light went out, yet it seemed as if she had been standing there for eternity. She knew from experience just how easy it was to become lost and disoriented in dark, unfamiliar places.

'I'm here. 'His voice sounded strangely distorted by the emptiness, echoing, richer. Relief flooded her and with it an excitement that was shocking in its intensity.

She was alone with him, beneath this structure of rock and stone, carved from the land centuries ago. Her flesh was reacting to it, desire prickling along her nerves and into her sex. The hunter and the hunted, but which was which? It was a primordial feeling that she couldn't explain.

'Is there something wrong with the candle?' It was as if she was fighting for survival, yet very aroused.

'No.' He spoke out of the stygian darkness.

'Then light it.'

'Do you really want me to?

This was ridiculous and had gone on long enough. She never went anywhere without a flashlight and fished it out of her pocket. His face swam into view, expressionless, calm, almost unnatural.

She tried to laugh, but it stuck in her throat. 'That's better,' she gasped.

'Don't tell me you were frightened, Freya? Not the intrepid explorer of ancient monuments?' The irony in his voice was challenging.

'Of course I wasn't frightened,' she bluffed. 'Just startled. That's all.'

'We'll go now. I won't bother with the candle as you have your torch.'

'Where's yours? You had it upstairs.' His body drew her like a magnet, but she didn't move towards him. She felt relief, yet was excited and aroused

'It's here.' It was in his hand and he swung the beam towards the steps.

'Then why didn't you switch it on?'

'So that you might experience what captives must have felt when the jailor went away, taking any light with him.'

She wanted to ask him why he needed to do this, but it seemed irrelevant. The strange episode was over, and it probably meant nothing. It left her feeling deflated and she was quiet until they reached the Great Hall again.

Then, 'Thank you, Maxwell,' she said calmly. 'I'll

discuss everything that I have seen with Mr Chalmers. He'll be in touch.'

'It's been a pleasure meeting you, Freya.' He was staring at her through his horn-rimmed glasses, and this seemed to put space between them. He walked with her to the outside steps, so cool, calm and collected, whilst she was in turmoil. She reached her car and looked back, but he had disappeared and the heavily studded door was shut.

The first thing she did on reaching home was plug in the kettle. She needed a cup of tea and a cigarette like never before. 'Bloody hell!' she said aloud as she got out a mug. 'He's a nut-case, or is it me?'

It was gone two and she gave Andrew a quick call. 'I've been and come back. Will be with you in an hour.'

'How did you get on with him?' His calm steadied her.

'No problem. I suppose you might say he's eccentric, but I can't see any difficulties.'

'Right. Catch you later.'

Hearing his voice had brought matters back into prospective. She was just being silly and imaginative. It was because she fancied Maxwell, but he hadn't reacted towards her as men usually did. What had she expected? He was famous and she nothing more than a means to free up his property. And even if he had shown more interest, did she really want to get entangled with him? There wasn't the slightest doubt that he would be more than just difficult. For all she knew he might be married, although she couldn't remember hearing anything about this through the media. She didn't do married men.

Hungry, she made herself a sandwich, then repaired her makeup and rehearsed what she was going to say to

Andrew. Nothing about the light failure in the dungeon. She'd skirt around this. Andrew was too perceptive and she didn't want to put him off, needing to talk to Moira about all this before she made any move.

Joan was in the office. 'How did it go?' she asked when Freya walked in.

'OK. Sinclair's a bit of a weirdo, but it'll work out.'

She scanned a couple of letters that lay on her desk, and then went to report to Andrew. He was so pleased to see her that she thought he was doing to kiss her, but he merely took her hand and gave her a chair opposite his. 'Was it all right?'

'Fine,' she answered, though her shrink had told her that this means "Fucked up. Insecure, Neurotic and Egocentric."

'And Sinclair?' He picked up the notes she handed over and flicked through them.

'It's difficult to tell after only one meeting, but he seems amenable and open to suggestions. The house is wonderful, so many interesting features.'

'We'll go together on the next visit.'

She didn't know whether to be glad or sorry, but recognized the wisdom of this, for the sake of the project if not herself. Deep down, she was anticipating a further tour with Maxwell, including the dungeon where goodness only knew what might happen. One thing was for sure—she'd wear a new pair of panties, the briefer the better. Gathering her wayward thoughts, she concentrated on telling Andrew all about Daubeney Manor.

The more she talked, the more enthusiastic she become. It truly was spectacular and packed full of interest. 'We're lucky to have the chance to examine it,' she concluded.

They had been lost in talk, unaware that the office staff was leaving. 'Why don't you come back to my place? I'll cook for us and we can go on planning,' he said.

She hesitated, but only for a second. Why not? She asked herself. Surely it would be better than going home alone, eating alone, watching telly, bored out of her skull? Carl would loom large in her memory and she would be tempted to get him on his mobile, humiliating herself by asking him to come back. Anything, rather than the crippling loneliness.

'Thank you. That would be nice,' she said, thinking of the packet of three in her bag. She was on the pill, but pregnancy was not the only hazard.

When with Carl, it had not been necessary, or so she had thought, though wasn't so sure now. In a spirit of bravado she had taken condoms from the depth of her lingerie drawer, telling herself she was now ready for anything that offered.

They left the building together. She followed Andrew in her car, mapping out her life in a different way. This time last week she would have been rushing home to cook for Carl. Who would be her next love? Would it be Andrew or maybe Maxwell or someone as yet unknown?

CHAPTER 3

The meal was delicious. They listened to music and Freya felt at home, but they were pussy-footing around. Then Andrew said outright, 'You asked me to stay last night. I've spent the day kicking myself for refusing.'

'Don't worry about it.' She was sitting with him in the depths of a leather settee. He hadn't settled until the dishwasher had been loaded and everything cleared away, not in the least impulsive, and this was both endearing and irritating.

'We don't have to go in early tomorrow.' His arm was resting along her shoulders and he edged closer.

'Mr Chalmers, are you suggesting that I sleep here?' Her mock reproach hid a multitude of feelings, one being weariness with the games consenting adults play and two, regret that she wasn't there with Maxwell.

'Yes, Miss Mullin, I am.' He was smiling at her and she relaxed, accepting the here and now, and not thinking of yesterday or tomorrow. There was only the present.

His kiss was tentative at first, but when she opened her lips to receive his probing tongue, he took over, feasting on her mouth, and she responded. He explored her breasts, lifted her vest top and ran a finger across her brassiere, teasing the nipples into even more prominence. Pleasure coursed through her. Maxwell had roused but confused her. Andrew's needs were simple, or so she thought.

Upstairs, she found a spare toothbrush, rinsed her mouth and then washed before entering the bedroom. It was the first time she had been anywhere but the ground floor and she was intrigued. It was sparse but comfortable, as one would expect of a bachelor pad. There were none of the little touches that a woman brings.

As if unable to believe his luck, Andrew had kept kissing her as they climbed the stairs, but now he seemed shy. Freya unhooked her earrings and removed her necklace, expecting him to fall with her into the bed and continue love-making. Instead he mumbled something about a shower and disappeared into the bathroom. Puzzled, yet flattered by his desire to be bandbox fresh for her, she stripped off her jeans and top, panties and bra, and climbed into his bed.

It was strange, a different feel to the valance and duvet, a different smell and a firmer mattress. Freya never slept well the first night away from home. As for sharing with a new man? She'd not done this since her student days . When she met Carl, she had been so bowled over and cock-struck that it has seemed the most natural thing in the world. She pulled the cover up under her chin and watched the door, surprised when Andrew appeared stark naked.

Either he was putting on an act or flaunting his tackle, but whatever he strode in positively and didn't pause until he stood before her. She had to admit that he certainly had something to be proud of. His cock was fully erect, a good nine inches of thick masculinity, springing from a nest of crisp brown hair. His body was trim, with wide shoulders and a slim waist, his hips taut and his thighs and legs well shaped. She controlled the urge to handle that uncircumcised projectile. It was a long time since she had seen an uncut penis. Carl's had been robbed of its foreskin. She wondered what Maxwell's was like.

Filled with a lust that was unusual for her, she yearned to sit on Andrew's and feel it penetrating deep inside.

Carl had sometimes complained that she was tepid. She had begun to wonder if he was the right man for her. Desire was there, flaming high at times, but needing to be stoked. Now she admitted that he hadn't come up to snuff lately. Would Andrew? There was only one way to find out.

'Are you going to stand there all night?' She grabbed him, pulling him into her embrace as she sat on the side of the bed, legs spread.

He lost his balance and tumbled back with her. Any reticence on his part vanished and he took over, pinning her down, feasting on her naked form, caressing her with hands and mouth. And, heaven be praised, he knew all about the clitoris. Familiar with it, one might say.

She moaned, squirmed, clung to him, rubbing against his fingers and lips. Control was slipping away, replaced with urgency, but common sense prevailed and she reached for her bag. His hand came down on hers.

'Don't worry.' He left her for a second, opening the bedside cabinet and taking out a silvery packet. 'Though, darling, there's nothing to worry about. I have a clean bill of health, and I can't say I'd be distressed if we made a baby together. In fact, I'd rather like it.'

Dear God! she thought. I do believe he's sincere!

It was all proceeding too smoothly. She wondered if she was one of those women who needed the challenge of bad behaviour on the part of their lovers, even a touch of violence and fear. There had been much more excitement and sheer animal lust when she had been in the dark with Maxwell.

She unwrapped a condom and set about the pleasurable task of preparing his rock-hard tool. First, she licked it from base to tip, concentrating on the flange, feeling him shudder and hearing his quick intake of breath. He was ready, and she tasted the milky juice that trickled from the eye. She took care not to tip him over the edge, reluctant to lose that first, violent rush of spunk. Slipping the rubber on from tip to base, she wished she didn't have to cover his delicious cock but, despite his words, one had to be sensible. They might not be on speaking terms tomorrow.

He lay beside her and she kept him waiting, working her tongue round his dark nipples, making him gasp. Pushing him flat on his back, she straddled him, lowering herself on to that powerful prong, taking him into her inch by slow inch. She faced him, staring into his eyes, seeing them glaze and knowing that she was in charge. He cupped her breasts, thumbs revolving on the tips. She pumped hard, up and down, then brought her hands round to spread her labia, fingers on her clit.

Andrew's hips were moving beneath her, driving his cock, and she knelt there, knees either side of him, open and vulnerable, massaging the head of her pleasure bud. She increased her motion, riding him desperately, her climax breaking, and he cried out, his cock throbbing inside her as he, too, reached his apogee.

She slid off him and he took the condom from his deflated penis, wrapped it in a tissue and dropped it to the floor, then eased the duvet over them and folded his arms around her. Even at such a moment his actions were precise and, though she cuddled up to his warm, naked body, still tingling from her orgasm, she was wondering if it would work between them.

Freya was almost dressed when Andrew looked across

at her. 'You're not going?' he mumbled, coming fully awake.

'It's almost two in the morning.' She sat on the bed to slip on her shoes.

'But…I thought…' he said, bemused.

'I have to go.' She leaned across and kissed him lightly, then gathered up her bag and jacket. 'I'll see you in the office later.'

With that she walked out, got into her car and drove home.

'It's not that I don't like him. I do.' Freya was on the phone to Moira, back from Bermuda. She had managed to catch her before she left for work.

'You don't have to explain to me, petal.' Moira said briskly. 'I'm glad you've got rid of that prick, Carl, and can understand you not wanting to take on another. Be free for a while. Enjoy what's on offer. Tell me more about Maxwell Sinclair.'

'You know of him?'

'Of course I do! Did an interview with him for *The Connoisseur* not long ago.'

'What did you think of him?'

'I'd give him breakfast.' This meant eight out of ten in Moira's reckoning of fuckability. 'Look, I've got to dash now. When can we meet up for a girly chat? What about tonight? I'll see you in *Charlie's* at eight. OK?'

'I've arranged a meeting with Sinclair tomorrow morning. He seemed pleased with your visit and is perfectly amenable to suggestions.' Andrew stood as Freya walked into his office. He smiled at her hesitantly.

'Fine. I'll prepare the paperwork I've done so far.' Including the dungeon? She asked herself. Yes, she'd touch on it briefly

She took a seat and crossed her knees, aware of her shapely calves in sheer sepia stockings. It would soon be warm enough to go bare-legged. Usually she wore jeans, particularly if her work entailed clambering about houses, but today an imp of perversity had urged her to dress up, rather then down. Though having doubts about her relationship with Andrew, she wasn't prepared to let him go, not just yet. One screw and a couple of dates were not enough on which to base judgement

He fidgeted, shuffled papers, chewed on his pen. It was amusing to see such a usually cool and collected man put off his stroke. 'Did you get home all right?' he asked.

'Yes.' She felt that she owed him some explanation. 'I like my own bed.'

'Ah, of course.' His face lit up. 'It was nothing to do with me, then?'

'No, indeed not.'

He pushed it a bit further. 'You're missing Carl, I suppose.'

'Not as much as I thought I would.'

'Then we can go out again? There's a concert at the town hall on Saturday. I thought about getting a couple of tickets. The Burlington Orchestra are playing Brahms and Mozart. Would you like to come?'

'Thank you. That would be lovely.'

I'm committing myself, she thought. What will Moira say?

Plenty, as it happened, when they sat over drinks in *Charlie's Bar* that evening.

After Freya told her about the concert, she started with, 'Why are you doing this?'

'He's nice. I've always got on well with him. Maybe it would have happened before if it hadn't been for Carl.'

'That little shit! I never could understand what you saw in him.'

Charlie's Bar was an establishment designed for the up and coming. Newly opened, it offered an alternative from the traditional hotels, restaurants and public houses that catered for Blackheath's general population. Once it had been a rundown pub, but Charlie, a landlady from London who had moved to the country, had seized the opportunity for a turn-around. She had kept the antique look,

beams, brass and candles, but encouraged a wider ranging clientele.

Freya could see people she knew through her job as well as musicians, artists and show folk who had settled in the picturesque town. Moira was eyeing one or two while she talked, having chosen a bar stool, glamorous in slim-fitting, boot-flared trousers, a tight sweater and flowing poncho. Paying little heed to the current vogue for straight, blonde hair, she encouraged her mane of long, auburn curls, emphasised her eyes with kohl and green shadow and outlined her generous mouth in scarlet. Not a natural redhead, her skinned tanned beautifully, golden from the Caribbean sun.

'It's just as well we don't go for the same blokes.' Freya perched beside her. Sometimes Moira's criticism hurt.

'It wouldn't take a rocket scientist to work that out. You go all soppy about them. I don't, but I love you all the same, you daft mare. Can you sneak me in to have a nose around Maxwell's gaff?"I don't know about that.

Maybe later, when I start work there, but Andrew is fussy about who we let in. Anyway, when will you be here?'

Moira led a hectic life, always in demand, jetting off on some glamorous consignment or another, film premieres, interviews with celebrities, keeping up with her columns in the glossies. Her schedule was packed.

'I can make time. An inside story about his latest project would be in demand. Don't worry. I'd

include you in it.' She was unscrupulous when it came to getting a scoop.

'I'll see how it goes.' Freya had known Moira for years. Though much younger than him, she had been Ray Mullin's mistress and helped Freya cope when he died. They were close.

When a mansion had been converted into luxury apartments in Blackheath , Moira had bought one to be near her. The town was within striking distance of Bristol Airport, Bath and Salisbury, and a two hour journey from London, very convenient for a journalist who wanted to be at the hub of activity, yet live in peaceful surroundings, though she had kept on her flat there. Freya could talk to her about most things, but her flamboyant life-style made her sometimes uneasy.

She changed the subject. 'How did you get on with Sarah's son?'

'Robbie? He's a babe. Thought himself experienced. Has had several girlfriends since being at university, but, my dear, he was hopeless until I trained him. Hadn't a clue. Imagined that the female came when he did. What a dork! Now he knows about the clit and will thank me for turning him into a good lover. I've done him a favour, but am tired of being the teacher. Need a guy who is into sex games.'

51

'Can't help you there, I'm afraid.' Though Freya had harboured suspicions that Carl was more interested in alternative love-play than he cared to admit, she had never experimented.

'Dear God! Don't tell me I have to go to London for it? There must be people out in the sticks who are up for fun that's a little bit different?' Moira cast an eye over the bar-tender. He was swarthy and Italian looking. 'See the way he handles that cocktail-shaker? I'd like to shake *his* cock for him. I'll bet he'd be up for a little punishment. A flick of the whip across his butt to make him obey my commands, and I'd keep him waiting before I let him spurt.'

Freya was too embarrassed to study Moira's next possible victim. She had already gone into action, engaging him in conversation. His knowing smile and smouldering eyes showed that he was not averse to whatever she was proposing. She glanced back at Freya and gave the thumbs up. Freya sighed; there was little chance now of monopolising her attention and getting the advice she sorely needed. Moira ordered another drink but Freya declined. She was driving.

'His name's Giovanni and he comes from Florence,' Moira informed her. 'We're meeting at eleven when he finishes his shift, so there's plenty of time to catch up on the gossip. Fill me in about these men of yours.'

It was good to talk, bringing everything into perspective. Freya realised she was worrying too much, letting it prey on her mind. 'Enjoy,' Moira insisted. 'Have fun. Play the buggers at their own game. That's what life's about, isn't it? You're too serious. Chill.'

Freya left Moira to wait for her stud to come off duty

when she said, 'That's Ok. He probably has a car. If not, I get a taxi back to my place.'

'Will you be all right? You don't know anything about him. Is it wise to take him home?'

'Stop worrying. I eat his sort for breakfast.'

'Well, if you say so, but I'll be on the end of the phone if you need me '

Freya still hadn't got used to entering her empty house. Maybe I should get a cat, after all, she thought, putting the chain on the front door. But no. Don't take on any more responsibilities. Follow Moira's advice and be free for a while. She picked up the cordless phone and took it up to bed with her, just in case her headstrong friend rang. She almost wished she would. Settled under the duvet with the television switched on, she flipped through the channels, hoping to see something that would lull her to sleep. It was terribly lonely, although she took comfort from the fact that if she rang Andrew he'd probably be over like a shot.

Maxwell was there to greet them. Large as life and twice as natural, Freya thought, knocked sideways by the force of his presence, his looks, his knowledge and his arrogance. Andrew paled in comparison, though he was obviously a much less complex person.

It was a sunny morning and she wore a cotton skirt, a loose jacket and sandals. Andrew had picked her up and the drive to the manor was pleasant. She refused to admit to herself that her heart was racing at the prospect of seeing Maxwell. And now, there he stood, casually dressed in chinos and a sweat-shirt, Hilary and Donna dancing attendance. Maxwell treated Freya like an old friend and Andrew was made welcome,

53

brief-case, officialdom and all. The two men were very polite, treating each other with studied courtesy, yet Freya thought that anyone with half an eye could see the tension between them. Both would want their own way when it came to decisions about Daubeney Manor. As far as she was concerned, this added a touch of piquancy to the situation

Usually the only thing remotely exciting about her job was the building itself, but now it had a lot more going for it; the rivalry of two good-looking men, both intent on coming out on top. Instinct told her that it was not merely the house that was likely to set them at logger-heads, but had a lot to do with her.

She recognised that Donna, too, had picked up on the vibes.

Hilary, meanwhile, fawned on Maxwell like a veritable lap-dog, and Andrew exchanged a quizzical glance with Freya, as much as to say, 'Who is this creep?'

This time they trotted after Maxwell as he took his visitors on a tour of inspection. He answered Andrew's questions succinctly. 'Jeffrey Plover is my architect, and he is bringing in a surveyor and builder to make any structural alterations, including the kitchen, extra bathrooms and a new central heating system. We thought solid fuel as opposed to oil.'

Andrew nodded. 'I would like to see Plover's proposals.'

They were standing in the kitchen and Maxwell unrolled sketches of the layout and spread it on the pine table. Andrew leaned over it and Maxwell explained what he wanted, and Freya was caught up in the different ambiences; Donna's feelings towards her boss, Hilary's need to be in on the act, and her own confused emotions. All this was not exactly conducive to a clear-sighted view of the alterations.

Andrew was perfectly calm, his usual controlled self, pointing out this and that to Maxwell and finally requesting to see the wine-cellar and any areas below. This was the moment Freya had been dreading, yet at the same time excitement sped through her and she would have liked everyone to disappear, save herself and Maxwell.

Andrew perused the cellar, making notes and offering suggestions and then came the moment when they descended even lower. Hilary and Donna lit candles and she was all of a twitter, and so was he. Maxwell held Freya's gaze, one brow raised questioningly, as if they shared a secret.

'Ah, the dungeons.' Andrew took the candle that Hilary lit and offered. 'How fortunate that they are still in existence.'

'It's a great talking point,' Maxwell agreed. 'And full of historic significance,'

'Have you considered opening the house to the public?' Andrew held Freya's hand to steady her down the twisting steps. 'I'm sure that local schools would jump at the chance to bring pupils here.'

'I may do just that.' Maxwell was at the bottom, looking back up at them, the candlelight planing his cheekbones and making his eyes shine.

'Firstly, we must insure that it's safe. Get your electrician to run cables down here.' Andrew was looking around with all the eagerness of the history buff. 'Don't you think this may spoil the atmosphere? I rather like the feeling that we are seeing it as some unfortunate prisoner did. Dark and gloomy and rather alarming. What do you think, Freya?'

It was the first time he had spoken to her directly. His voice took her off guard. There was a wealth of hidden meaning in his apparently harmless question. It brought back the moment when she had been alone with him in the darkness.

'You may be right,' she managed to answer, but Andrew broke in.

'We have to be aware of safety. You need to take out insurance and make it as easy as possible for people to view it without coming to harm.'

'You're right, Mr Chalmers,' Donna piped up. 'I find it really spooky, and I'm sure school- children might.'

Hilary gave a nervous laugh. 'In my experience, they like being spooked. I must admit that it sends shivers down my spine.'

Andrew went round, tapping walls, viewing damp areas, and scribbling notes. 'It seems sound enough. Your surveyor will assess it. And is this the lowest part of the foundations?'

Maxwell nodded, 'As far as I'm aware.'

Freya wanted nothing more than to leave. It wasn't that it was steeped in dismal memories, a prison where men had suffered torture and incarceration. She had entered such places before, more often than not entirely alone, and they hadn't affected her. It was Maxwell who was causing mayhem in her emotions. Not only her, by the look of it. He affected both Donna and Hilary, and it was hard to be sure if this was because he was their boss, or for personal reasons.

Andrew seemed unaffected, doing his job calmly. 'I'd like to have a chat with Plover.'

'Donna, give him Jeffrey's phone number and e-mail address,' Maxwell said, then added, 'Perhaps you and Freya would like to come to dinner one evening and I'll get Jeff to come along.. Shall we say Friday?'

Both agreed and nothing could have been more affable. Andrew seemed pleased, but Freya couldn't shake off that feeling of unease as they drove away from the manor.

Alone in his study, Maxwell sat in his operator's chair before the wide, cluttered desk holding his computer, printer, reference books and all the tools of the writer's trade. No matter where he decided to live, there was always a similar room where he could retire to work. He demanded peace and quiet and the adoring Donna was only permitted entrance when he had letters to dictate, manuscripts to send as attachments to his publishers, and e-mails to answer.

She had an office of her own where the day-to-day economics of his households were sorted. Thus he was freed from banks and bills and all the other dull matters that had to be coped with. Maxwell looked upon this as his right, always had done, even from a tiny child born to wealthy, influential parents.

He picked up the phone and dialled a number. It was mid-afternoon and knowing Jeffrey's habits, there was a good chance that he might catch him at home. He was about to hang up before the answer-machine clicked in, when the architect said, 'Hello, Jeff Plover here.'

'It's me … Maxwell.'

'Hi! How's it going up at the Big House?'

'OK. I don't see too many problems with the British Historic people. Rather the contrary, as it happens.'

'Ah, one of them is female, I take it.' Jeff chuckled and

Maxwell heard him say to someone in the room. 'Maxwell's got another pussy to stroke.'

'I didn't tell you that.' Maxwell was amused. Jeff knew him only too well. 'Who've you got there, you dirty old sod?'

Jeff's voice was replaced by another's. 'It's me. Lola. How are you?'

Maxwell could see her in his mind's eye. Lola Descartes, model and tart. One of the raciest women on the scene. 'I'm all right. Have you any clothes on?'

'No. You interrupted us, sweetie. We were having it off. A little siesta, if you know what I mean.'

He did indeed. Lola was a dominatrix, among other occupations. A girl who had shagged her way to the top, using her beauty and immorality to become a celebrity. He had helped her along the way and she was game for anything he might suggest. It was a bonus to find her with Jeff. Thus he could kill two birds with one stone.

'Lola, I want you and Jeff to come to dinner. It's time you saw the manor and I need to win over the historic boffins so that they'll agree to my plans.'

'Darling,' she purred. 'You know I'd do anything for you. I'm remembering how we screwed. My clit is tingling and I'm going to rub it. Why don't you get out your cock and make it big. We could see who comes first. Jeff could join in, too and we'll have a race.'

It was very tempting and Maxwell could feel his erection chaffing against the inside of his pants. He placed his free hand on it, making it even larger, then unzipped, freeing the serpent. He could hear Lola breathing fast, and Jeff's lewd comments in the background.

It was irresistible, his cock sliding through his fingers, the foreskin stretched back from the helm. Jism seeped from the single eye. 'Lola,' he growled. 'Are you nearly there?'

'I am, pet, and so is Jeff.'

That lovely woman with her big breasts, long legs, and unabashed sexuality. He wished she was with him, using her hands and mouth expertly. Even the thought of this was bringing him to the point of no return. Then there was a tap at the door.

'Who is it?' he barked, angry and frustrated.

'It's Donna, sir. I have a message for you.'

'Damn!' he swore, then spoke into the phone. 'Look here, Lola, I want you and Jeff to come to dinner on Friday night. Ring me back later.'

He put down the receiver and tried to ease his cock back into his chinos, but it was useless. 'Come in, Donna,' he ordered. He kept his back to her as she entered, then swung round and she gasped at the sight. 'Get over here.'

When she reached him, he grabbed her and forced her to lie across the desk, lifting her skirt high and pushing aside her panties. This wasn't the first time that she had willingly relieved his sexual tension, and he slammed into her, while she whimpered and gasped and told him that she loved him.

CHAPTER 4

Freya was rooting through her wardrobe. 'What the hell am I going to wear? I've lost it completely since Carl went. No confidence in my own judgement.'

'Oh, come on! That's bull-shit and you know it. You've always had a flare. Don't try and kid me otherwise,' Moira said from the bed where she was relaxing among the pillows. 'My God, that Giovanni! At it like a rabbit all night long! I didn't get a wink of sleep!'

'Stop boasting. You know you loved every minute of it.' Freya dragged a purple velvet two-piece from its hanger and held it up against her. 'What about this?'

'There's too much of it. You want to show off your assets.'

Moira propped herself up on one elbow and stared at her in a way that she found disconcerting. It was like being studied by a man. She felt the need to cover herself, instead of standing there in her bra and thong. She'd heard rumours that Moira was bi-sexual, but had never put it to the test.

She reached for another dress. This was of chiffon with a calf-length pointed skirt and skimpy top. It had been an impulse buy when she was feeling low after a row with Carl about some girl he had paid far too much attention at a party. She had never worn it, but maybe now was the opportunity.

'I like it.' Moira got up and came over to her. 'Get it on and give us a twirl.' Freya did so, popping it over her head and wriggling her shoulders into it.

'Oh, damn! My bra shows.'

'Wear a strapless one,' Moira advised, pacing round her critically. 'It's cool A show-stopper. I like the jagged hem and the way it clings to your thighs before swirling out. You need high heels and dark stockings and suspenders. All the men will be getting boners. Are there any other girls invited?'

'I don't know. Maxwell only mentioned his architect, Jeffrey Plover.'

'That leaves Maxwell and Adrew panting after you, and possibly this Jeff bloke as well.'

'You're incorrigible.' Freya rummaged in her lingerie drawer for a brassiere without straps. She found a black one and changed into it. 'Andrew tells me to pack an overnight bag. Apparently Maxwell has suggested that we stay, thus avoiding the choice between drinking and driving. I don't much like the idea of sleeping under his roof, or anyone else's for that matter.'

'Go for it, darling. Fling in a sexy nightie.'

'I don't own a sexy nightie. They're terribly old-hat. I sleep in the nude, or a long tee-shirt.'

'You've no sense of adventure.'

Freya was aware of a frisson as Moira helped, arms coming around from the back where she had been adjusting the fastening, hands cupping her breasts. Freya had never made love with a woman and had thought herself completely straight, but now she began to wonder. Her nipples responded to that feminine touch and her womb ached, just as it did when a man caressed her.

Moira's eyes met hers in the dressing-table mirror, amused and knowing. 'Darling, if you ever feel like getting on the other bus, call me.'

Made uncomfortable by her own reactions, Freya pulled away and hurried over her preparations. Moira reverted to her former sisterly self, helping to wind her hair into a chignon, wishing her luck, and then leaving to meet Giovanni. It was his evening off and she had several surprises planned for him.

Freya scrutinised herself in the pier-glass. She liked what she saw. The dress was near perfect for the occasion. The flower-print pattern of the diaphanous fabric worn over a black slip, suited her fair skin and hair. Moira had advised on make-up and she had applied more than usual, feeling glamorous and ready for anything. She almost wished she was going alone, yet was glad that Andrew would be there to protect her. From whom? she mused. Back came the answer—from yourself.

'Max, how did you find such a place? Jesus! It'll be great for gatherings. You're own personal Hell Fire Club,' Lola exclaimed.

'That's what I thought, but you're not to say a word about it. Do you understand?' His grip on her tightened, thrilling her to the core.

'Of course I won't. This will be our secret. You know me, darling. I love secrets. Wow! What a spot! A fancy grotto, great for fun and games.'

The whole ambience was exactly what turned her on, hidden underground, holding mysteries from the past. It was filled with flickering light from candles in floor-standing girandoles. The flames cast a ruddy glow over walls decorated with paintings and naked statues.

'I've studied follies,' he went on. 'Visited a few already unearthed, then came across references to one rumoured to have existed in the West Country. Daubeney Manor was mentioned I thought no more about it until it came on the market.'

'And you bought it, investigated and found what you were searching for.'

'Too right I did. It wasn't in bad shape. Someone, a former owner I imagine, had kept it in good order for his or her own amusement. The paintings are of the time when I think this was constructed.. The surveyors and solicitors knew nothing of its existence, but I found the entrance concealed beneath this mock temple built in the eighteenth century.'

'It's quite luxurious. No sign of damp or mould.'

'I've cleaned it up, and it's ventilated and has another entrance.'

'Where?'

'You're asking too many questions. Accept that it's here for our use. That's all you need to know. Once the British Heritage people have stopped sniffing around, we can invite friends down to stay in the manor and use our exclusive facilities, offering this as a venue where they can act out their fantasies. At a price, of course.'

'So this is the reason you brought me into the grounds? I wondered if you fancied an outdoor screw.'

He chuckled. 'That, too. I have yet to christen it.'

Lola's skin prickled. He was the most exciting lover she had ever had. Cool, urbane, highly intelligent and knowledgeable, she had been his from the first time he had fucked her, hidden behind the bushes at a television producer's garden party. And this was Lola, top-model and celebrity, who had prided herself on being no man's slave.

He was a complex being. Sometimes charming, at others vile tempered, but no one fulfilled her like he did. Even when he was being tender there was an underlying hint of savagery. Now he had her pressed against one of the walls, her bodice pushed down to her waist, breasts bare while he nipped at her flesh. Heat tingled to her loins, and the gusset of her panties was wet. She had learned through bitter experience not to ask for what she wanted. He could be perverse and would probably do the opposite — harsh when she needed gentleness — tender if she craved brutality. He was a law unto himself.

The stone was cold against her bare back, and his arms caged her on either side, his mouth taking possession of hers. She could tell that he wanted to be rough, yet was determined to prolong the agony. OK, Maxwell, she thought. Two can play at that game. Her hand shot down between them and grasped his balls through his trousers.

He pulled back. She freed her lips and whispered, 'Worried I might damage your crown jewels, Max? Would I do that to you?'

In answer, he unzipped, releasing his cock and her fingers closed round it, palm registering the heat and hardness. He still held her with one arm, but his free hand trailed down to hitch up her skirt and inveigled his fingers into her thong. Her pubis was swept clean of hair, and he twirled the little gold ring that pierced her right labia, then started to massage her clitoris.

Frightened that he might decide to torment her, withdrawing that electrifying touch, she pressed against his fingers, moving her pubis up and down, starting to feel the beginning of orgasm, a force that couldn't be stopped. She shuddered as the bliss coursed through her, arching against him as it

peaked and then faded. He slid his hands under her buttocks and lifted her. She clamped his neck in a stranglehold and scissored her legs about his waist as he slid his erection into her.

He was so close to the edge that it took only a few frantic strokes to bring him to orgasm, his semen caught by the black rubber that she didn't recall him putting on. Recovering quickly, he pulled away from her and set her down on her feet. She staggered on her stiletto heels, then steadied herself and adjusted her clothes. But still she wanted more, yearning to remain with him in their hideaway.

'I must go.' He moved towards the entrance. 'The other guests will be arriving.'

'Not yet, please, Max. I'm sure the devoted Donna will cover your tracks . Does she know about this?'

'No. Only you and I. Make sure you keep it that way until I tell you otherwise.'

The note in his voice made her shiver. Maxwell didn't take kindly to betrayal, as several mutual acquaintances had discovered to their cost.

The manor was at its gracious best, a perfect spot in which to entertain. Freya left her wrap and case in the bedroom to which she had been conducted and, carrying her clutch-bag, went down to join those gathered in the Great Hall.

She found Andrew, looking smooth in a dinner jacket, and murmured, 'What a lovely house! I wish it was mine.'

He smiled at her as she slipped her hand in the crook of his elbow. 'You'd have to win the lottery to afford it, and its upkeep. My room is just across the way from yours unless, of course, you'd like me to pop in and keep you company.'

She had no time to answer, though the question had been on her mind. Maxwell came across to join them. He was wearing black; black suit, black shirt and black tie. It made him taller and slimmer and even more desirable. 'Welcome, both. Come and meet the others.'

Jeffrey Plover greeted Andrew warmly. 'Hello there. Long time no see. How are tricks? Are they keeping you busy?' Music played in the background, sophisticated jazz suitable for the occasion. Jeffrey took Freya's hand and bowed over it. 'So, you are Andrew's colleague. Lucky him.'

He was a rotund man with reddish hair and an engaging manner. The woman with him came as a surprise. Freya found herself being introduced to a slim creature wearing the very latest vogue, with a red satin Basque and wrap-over skirt. Her legs seemed to go on forever, accentuated by the highest of heels. She had straight blonde hair with fashionably dark roots, cut in a spiky style that fell forward over her brow and ears and trailed around her neck and bare shoulders.

'I'm Lola Descartes.' Her voice was sweet and mellow.

'*The* Lola Descartes? I've seen you on television.' Freya was nonplussed. What other surprises was Maxwell about to spring?

The next left her practically speechless. A rangy young man stepped forward, .looking rather out of place in formal dress. As she recalled, he had been an untidy individual.

'Well, I'll be damned!' he exclaimed, gazing at her with keen blue eyes. 'If it isn't Freya Mullin.'

'Grant Foster.'

'How many years is it since we were at uni?'

'Too many. What are you doing here?'

'I was called in to see that the old place isn't about to fall down. I'm a structural engineer, among other things.'

'Funny we haven't met before in this game.'

'I've been abroad —America, Canada, Dubai.'

'That would account for it.' Freya was pleased to see

him. They had been in the same year at Bristol University, studying the same subjects. There had never been other than friendship between them, though it had come close once or twice, then he moved away and they lost touch.

He was a rugged-looking individual, tall and broad-shouldered, with shaggy, brown-gold hair that straggled to his collar. His looks had improved with maturity. Was he married? She glanced at his left hand but there was no wedding-ring. He apparently had the same thought.

'Is your husband here?'

'I don't have a husband.' This was getting too personal and she made sure he shook hands with Andrew, extricating herself and leaving them to building talk.

'Max tells me that you're one of those clever women who know all about old houses,' Lola said. Freya's hackles rose at her patronising attitude. So, Maxwell had been discussing her, had he? What had he said? And what was this woman to him?

'It's my job.' She went to turn away.

Lola placed a hand on her arm. 'It must be fascinating. Have you read any of Max's books? I couldn't put them down.'

'I wouldn't have thought you a great reader.' Was she envious of Lola? Freya admitted that she was. So gorgeous a woman, and obviously one of Maxwell's intimates.

'You'd be surprised, darling.' Lola raised her eyebrows and gave a smile that could have meant nothing or everything.

'Dinner is swerved,' announced the butler from the doorway.

Freya assumed this to be Armitage, Danny's mother's beau, and followed him as he led the way into the next room. This proved to be the place for formal meals, as Maxwell had explained to her on her first visit. It was delightful, with original panelling hung with portraits of former owners dating back to the time of Queen Elizabeth. The marble fireplace was filled with dried rhododendron blossoms She wondered what had happened to the family, forcing them to part with all this. Some financial disaster, perhaps? An addiction to gambling? This had been the downfall of many an aristocratic.

The mahogany dining-table was set with silver; candlesticks and flower-vases, glittering cutlery and sparkling glass. Freya and Lola were the only ladies present and their chairs were pulled back for them by menservants. These also waited at table, under the auspices of Armitage. Maxwell took his place at the head, with Lola on one side and Freya on the other.

The first course arrived. Wine was poured. 'I called in caterers.' Maxwell was the perfect host, seeming to enjoy entertaining. 'The kitchen is as yet unusable. Not for long, I hope,' and he cocked an eyebrow at Freya and raised his long-stemmed glass.

'We'll do what we can to hurry it up,' Andrew interjected. He was on her right side, next to Grant, with Jeffrey opposite.

Because it was a small gathering, only part of the lengthy board had been used, producing an intimate atmosphere. They could have been close friends instead of business associates. The conversation covered several topics, including politics, music and the arts. Maxwell was well up in all these and Andrew held his own. Grant seemed a little out of his depths and Freya tried to talk with him, though hindered by Andrew sitting between them. She wanted to know more about what he had done with his life since they parted. He seemed more grounded than the others.

Lola was proving to be something more than just a pretty face, well versed in the latest happenings at home and abroad. Freya felt dwarfed by her, retreating into her shell. As for Maxwell? He was including Freya in the general talk, and her spirits lifted a little, but when she dropped her bag and bent to retrieve it, she gazed under the table at the astonishing sight of Lola's hand at his crotch. Both of them were carrying on talking as if nothing untoward was taking place, his tone as level as ever, in spite of a large erection. Freya sat up and reached for her wine, trying to stem the jealous anger that rushed through her.

Dessert arrived and, although it was a faultless concoction, she had little appetite. It was easier to keep drinking and her glass seemed to be constantly replenished. The voices around her became louder, or so it appeared. Eventually they all rose, taking coffee in the drawing-room, where a black Steinway grand piano took pride of place.

'Does anyone here play?' Maxwell asked.

'Oh, don't be so modest, Max,' carolled Lola. 'You know you're an expert.'

He spread his hands and shrugged apologetically. 'I'm horribly out of practice. No time.' But he ran his fingers over the keys, then perched on the stool before the gleaming instrument.

The chatter ceased, silenced by the notes that rippled through the room. The guests settled in armchairs or on couches, glasses to hand. Freya recognised the music. 'It's a Chopin *Nocturne*,' she whispered to Andrew. He nodded.

Max's rendition was of concert pianist standard, and she listened, enthralled. The romantic in her responded to the sight of this handsome man absorbed in the composer's work, reproducing it without a flaw. It was a magical moment, affecting her more than when she had been in his company going over the house for the first time and being with him in the dungeon. There were depths to him that never appeared on the surface. She wanted to delve into them, almost moved to tears by his superlative playing.

Spontaneous applause followed the second's pause as the final notes drifted away. 'That was great!' Lola enthused. 'Did Chopin compose that before, during or after his affair with George Sands, the woman writer?'

'I've no idea. Does it matter?' He rose impatiently, expressing annoyance at her mentioning mundane matters. 'It's his music that counts. The private life of a genius is neither here nor there. He died young, and they say that the flame of inspiration is so bright that it can burn out the recipient.'

'Will you play again?' Freya was unable to resist going over to him.

'Later, perhaps.' He seemed uneasy at having shown his sensitive side. 'Come now, drink up, everyone. How about a game of cards?'

'Can I come in with you?' Andrew leaned against the wall near her bedroom door, an arm around her. He was more than a little drunk, his hair ruffled, his speech slurred.

'I don't think that's a good idea.' She was not entirely sober herself. Maxwell had insured that his guests were well supplied, the evening becoming rowdy, finishing up with dancing the salsa to South American rhythms booming from his superb stereo system.

'Remember how we used to do this at college parties?' Grant had said at one point, leading her effortlessly through the steps. He always had been a good dancer.

'I remember.' She had wished they could go on, but Lola butted in, wanting to monopolise his attention. Freya hoped she didn't succeed in shagging him, though telling herself not to be an arse. It was nothing to do with her.

Andrew *was*, however, but she didn't really want to share her bed with him.. 'I've had a bit too much to drink and have a stinking headache. I'll see you in the morning.'

'Don't forget our date for tomorrow evening. The concert. Remember?'

He kissed her unsteadily and staggered in the direction of his room. Freya let herself into hers and locked the door behind her. She could always open it if he came knocking in the small hours. She was rather too out of it to appreciate the décor, and simply climbed the narrow steps that ran round the four-poster and flopped across the mattress, pulling the quilt over her. There was a lamp burning on the side table, but she closed her eyes, controlling the whirling sensation and sinking into a deep sleep.

Later, she was never sure what woke her into darkness. Maybe it was someone breathing close by. 'Is that you, Andrew?' She faltered, then knew it was unlikely. The door was locked on the inside.

There was no reply, only the sound of someone drawing breath. She could smell the person now, and it wasn't a female, a combination of aftershave and brandy. There was a man in her room. His presence sent fear welling up, but at the same time she was strangely aroused. Was it Maxwell or Grant or even Jeffrey? They had all been flirting with her. But how had they gained entrance?

She decided to turn it into a joke. 'Oh, come, whoever you are. I know we're all pissed but what is this? A bet or something?'

Again silence, and the fear started to take root. She flung back the quilt and swung her legs over the side of the bed. Hands prevented her. Strong, steady hands. This was no drunk chancing his arm and carrying out some stupid male challenge. 'See if you can fuck her, mate. Get into her room, but you'll have to bring back proof. Fifty quid says you can't do it.'

She was still dressed and glad of it, though he started to caress her, large hands moving over the column of her throat and down to her breasts. It occurred to her to scream for help, but this seemed foolish and cowardly, besides which part of her wanted him to go on as she became more and more convinced that it was Maxwell. Her fingers encountered his face, but met leather. He was masked and, as she explored further, it was to find that this revenant who haunted the night was clad entirely in this soft, smooth substance.

Just for a second, reason abandoned her and she was chilled through and through as she wondered if it was indeed some demon trapped between the universes. She dismissed this. She didn't believe in ghosts. Or did she?

'Maxwell, is that you?' She managed to ask in a squeaky voice.

There was no reply, but he was on her and over her, bearing her back against the pillows. His weight was stifling, then he eased off and she felt him lift her skirt and brush aside her tanga. He found her epicentre and she cried out at the riveting feeling of his lips on her

72

clitoris, fingers spreading her labia wide. The combination of fear and sexual pleasure was so strong that it robbed her of strength.

She wanted to fight him off, but the idea that it was Maxwell made her helpless to do other than accept that skilled caress. He sucked at her bud, nipped at and pleasured it, and she writhed against his mouth, climax rising inside her, flooding through her cortex and along her nerves until nothing mattered but that she shatter into release.

It broke with such force that she blacked out for a second. He continued to smooth her swollen nubbin, but gently now and she felt him withdrawing. Expecting him to enter her, she was aware of plunging disappointment as his warmth vanished. She sat up feeling about for him, then switched on the bedside light.

The room was empty. Whoever or whatever had given her such intense pleasure had disappeared.

Freya sat there stunned, then got up and searched everywhere but there was no sign of him. Had it been Maxwell? The more she thought about it the more convinced she became. The door was firmly locked, the key still inserted from her side of it. He must have used a secret passage to gain entrance to her room and had probably planned it all along when he invited her and Andrew to stay overnight. Anger started to boil inside her. She couldn't even accuse him of rape for she had enjoyed the experience and he had not even penetrated her. Her sex felt swollen and wet, but this had been induced by him for her pleasure alone. What had he got out of it? Back came the answer and she almost wished she hadn't made a study of human behaviour. Maxwell was a control freak.

Like any first-class hotel, the guest rooms were equipped with the mechanics for tea or coffee making. Still trembling from the encounter, she switched on the kettle and found tea-bags, milk and sugar. She wandered to the window and pulled back the curtains a chink. It was still dark outside and she wondered how on earth she was to face Maxwell over breakfast. There was little doubt in her mind that her night visitor had been him.

CHAPTER 5

'I trust you slept well, Freya?' Maxwell was all smooth charm. Sunshine poured in at the breakfast room windows and nothing could have been more normal.

'Not too well. I never do in a strange bed. In fact, I had a nightmare.' She outdid him in politeness.

'I'm sorry to hear that. Perhaps it was the drink. I hope you'll feel more at home next time.'

Was there to be a 'next time'? What did he have in mind? She was annoyed with herself for the shiver of anticipation that ran down her spine.

Jennie Barker and Armstrong had been recruited to prepare and serve the meal. The sideboard contained a choice of cereals, bacon and eggs, toast and tea or coffee. Not all the guests had come down. Lola was absent, to Freya's relief. So was Jeffrey. Grant was bright-eyed and bushy-tailed, Andrew sober and collected, and Maxwell as calm as if he had never stolen into a lady's room under cover of darkness, brought her to orgasm and then left.

Perhaps he hadn't? In the bright light of day she wasn't convinced. She cursed him under her breath. He made her feel acutely uncomfortable and she didn't like it. Somehow, it seemed to give him a hold over her. Breakfast finished, they said goodbye, promising to repeat the experience some time soon. The only person she regretted leaving was Grant, though she couldn't be sure if he had fucked Lola or not.

'Let's keep in contact, and I'll see you around the manor anyway once we've been given the go ahead,' he said, as they exchanged business cards.

'Well, that was interesting, wasn't it?' Andrew

remarked from behind the wheel, driving back to Blackheath. 'Sinclair's an odd-ball.'

The last thing she wanted was to discuss their host, very nearly wondering if she had dreamed the strange incident. But there was no way could she tell him about it. He dropped her off at her house. She fished in her bag for the keys. 'I'll see you tonight for the concert.'

'I'll be here at seven. Ok?' He seemed reluctant to leave, as if hoping she would ask him in, but she needed to be alone.

I can't be all that keen on him, or else I'd be bonking him mindless at every opportunity, she thought, going up to unpack and change. There was plenty of time before the concert and she rang Moira, but got the answer-phone. She was probably still in bed with her Italian — or someone else. Freya made a shopping list and got into her car. There were vehicles parked outside every house in the street, for they had been built in the days when families didn't have their own transport only, perhaps, the humble push-bike, travelling on foot, by train or omnibus. Freya had looked into the possibility of having a garage built around the back, but space was limited.

There was nothing for it but taking the risk, leaving her car outside her front door and hoping the vandals would ignore it. She had been lucky so far, apart from having the tyres let down and a wing mirror smashed. If she had had her way she would have brought back public flogging or the stocks for young offenders. Depraved because they were deprived? Bollocks! Why couldn't they all be like Danny?

She was tired and edgy and her head ached as the result of too much alcohol. Shopping was a chore. There was no fun in cooking for herself. She filled the super-market trolley with frozen meals-for-one that could be heated in the microwave. Though she had Maxwell after her and Andrew, too, she needed to be part of a couple, despite her career and apparent independence. When she got home and had stowed her goods in the freezer, she flopped on the bed and fell asleep.

Maxwell was alone Everyone had gone, leaving him to his contemplations. The ancient world fascinated him. As a boy he had come across books in his father's library about Egypt and Greece, the Druids and old religions. He had never looked back, making a study of these at university. It had become his life work. He had acquired fame and money, but had a niggling ambition to find something really astonishing, equivalent to the discovery of the Saxon burial site at Sutton Ho.

He had shown Lola a part of his find, but not all. He followed his instinct, certain there was more hidden away. Giving Donna and Hilary strict orders that he was not to be disturbed, he retired to his study. There he equipped himself with a miners' lamp, a tool-bag, a pocket torch and a map of the underground ways that he had unearthed so far. The manor was a rabbit-warren of hidden passages and he was having an exhilarating time discovering them. As Lola had remarked there was nothing he and she liked more than secrets.

He knew it was likely to be cold and damp down there, so wore jeans, a sweater and an anorak, along with sensible boots. He was skilled at exploration and had a mobile with him, just in case there was an accident and he needed to contact the upper world. He had one regret: Freya wasn't there. Later, he promised himself. If it suits me to do so, I may share it with her. Though intent on his purpose, his thoughts flashed back to last night and his penis thickened as he remembered her response to her dark, demonic lover. He could almost smell her arousal as he brought on her climax. So wet, so hot for him, and he had restrained the urge to penetrate her, going back to his own room, via another passageway. There his hand had become his mistress.

He controlled himself, dwelling on his present adventure. He had managed to meet the last remaining descendent of the family who should have inherited the manor, had he not drunk all the remaining money away. Maxwell had succeeded in wheedling information from him for the price of several pints of beer, followed by whiskey chasers. This man had betrayed his forebears, and even sketched out tunnels hidden in the walls and grounds, once used as priest-holes or escape routes during wars and religious persecution. Maxwell's expertise had made it fairly easy for him to find these unrecorded ways.

The library, now his study, was lined with bookshelves containing many volumes that had come with the house. Not all, for many had been sold to pay off debts. He had been told where to find a small lever disguised as part of the ornamentation. When pressed, a section of the wall opened wide enough for a man to wriggle through and close after him.

Maxwell had visited there several times and after negotiating steps and narrow passages, he knew he would come out in the grotto beneath the folly. With a final glance around to make quite certain he was unobserved, he let himself through. Darkness enfolded him. He switched on the miner's lamp and its shaky beam guided him down.

Excitement carried him forward, an almost orgasmic thrill. This was his property, his discovery. Maybe he'd find a treasure unbeknown for centuries. His name would go down in the archives as the man who had unearthed it. This was what he yearned for above money, fame and the satisfaction of his sexual appetites.

He reached the spot where he had taken Lola. He could have lit the candles but decided against it, the lamp and torch would suffice. . If his calculations were right, then he wouldn't be there long. Steps yawned upwards, connecting with the folly. Maxwell moved carefully, tapping walls and pillars, searching for what he wasn't sure, though convinced there was more, much more, if only he could be patient. Along with most of his brethren in archeology, he was painstaking in his approach, going over every inch. Nothing.

He sat on the stone flags and reached in his knapsack for a thermos flask. Coffee might sharpen his wits. Sipping, his eyes roamed the ceiling, floor and walls once again and he noticed a slight discrepancy on the right of the steps. He alerted and flashed his torch, having abandoned the miners' lamp temporarily. Yes, there was no mistake. He had spotted a crack that would have escaped all but the keenest observer.

Moving closer, he implemented the torch light with the lamp, setting it on a ledge. Even so, the feature that had struck him as strange was hard to figure out. His sensitive fingers followed the crevice. He became sure that it was no geological fault, but man-made. He was sweating, fighting for control, telling himself that this was probably nothing. He persevered, becoming more certain that this concealed an opening of some sort. He worked away the incrustation, using his nails, steel-wool and a brush, but carefully. The last thing he wanted was to inflict damage in any way. His hands were bleeding. He took no notice.

At last the heavy stone yielded. He kept it steady, then lowered it to the ground. Another followed and there was space enough for him to look into the opening and shine the torch. A passage yawned ahead. He wriggled through and landed on solid flooring. The torch beam lit the darkness and he walked on until he met a blank wall. This time the bricks were not so firmly fixed and, determined to see what they concealed, he worked eagerly, as he had done before. At last he removed several, revealing an aperture beyond. His head was at an awkward angle and the torch's beam didn't go far, but what he managed to glimpse was unbelievable.

'My God!' he whispered, awestruck. 'This is how Carter must have felt when he opened Tutankhamen's tomb!'

No matter how troubled and out of sorts Freya might be, music always had a calming effect. The concert was no exception, The Burlington Orchestra well-known and popular, and the town hall filled to capacity. Andrew had booked good seats, and they arrived in time to purchase programmes and

exchange comments with other music lovers. She had dressed casual-smart for the occasion, and felt at ease. Andrew wore a lightweight suit and she was happy to have him as her escort.

Seated beside him, she became absorbed in the music, a Mozart symphony first, then the interval, followed by Brahms. Neither of these composers roused deep emotions within her, unlike the operas of Puccini and Wagner, but they soothed her and rekindled her faith in human kind. She had long ago decided that music came from somewhere beyond. If she ever doubted the existence of a supreme being, then listening to these sublime sounds made her think again. Where did the inspiration arise if it wasn't from divine realms? It brought her thoughts back to Maxwell and the way he had played the Chopin Nocturne. He had changed, losing his hard edge and becoming a vehicle for the Polish composer's gift.

After the appreciative applause that brought the show to a close, she walked out into the night with Andrew, still lost in dreams. He, too, was silent, as if contemplating his own soul, and it wasn't until they reached her house and found somewhere to park, that he spoke.

'The orchestra were very good, weren't they? Certainly lived up to their reputation.'

'They did indeed.'

'I don't know about you, but I find the earlier composers much more satisfying than the modern ones. I tried to get into an opera from Covent Garden put out on the TV the other night. It was the premier performance of a new work, and I turned it off after a while. It was so discordant. On the other hand, I used to find Bartok difficult but have learned to like his music. I taped the opera and will watch it again. Maybe you'd like to join me. We could make an evening of it.'

'Maybe.' Freya nodded, slipped the key into the lock and went inside. He followed. 'Coffee?' she asked.

'I'd rather take you to bed.'

His sudden boldness startled her. It was out of character. Was it the influence of the music? She didn't stop to question him or examine her own reactions, simple led the way upstairs.

Her bedroom, a precious retreat that she had shared with Carl. Did Andrew realise how privileged he was to be invited there? They were both cold stone sober, simply fired by the music. He held her, kissed her, and there was nothing harsh or demanding about his embrace. It was loving and tender, the element that she had longed to feel with Carl, but had never achieved. She responded, though unable to fathom why it didn't excite her. The revenant had caused far more mayhem in her loins, part terror, wholly sexual.

She redoubled her efforts, stripped for him, went down on him, happy to give him pleasure, while her hormones remained unmoved. 'Oh, darling, you're a wonderful lover,' he gasped, pulling away from her mouth in time to stop himself coming. 'Let me do it to you, and then maybe we can finish together.'

Spread-eagled on the duvet, she relaxed, giving herself over to purely bodily sensations. She knew from their previous love-making that he wouldn't leave her unsatisfied. Unemotionally, like a man being served by a prostitute, she welcomed his tongue on her clitoris and the way he sucked it gently between his lips. His fingers, meanwhile, spread her labia, while one probed her vagina. The feeling was delicious, and Freya's every nerve responded and that ache started in her womb, spreading, connecting with her spine and brain. Pleasure, pure and unadulterated, swept through her, the waves building until they suffused her with rainbow coloured light and feeling so intense that it almost resembled pain.

She shuddered, sighed and relaxed. He held her in his

arms, murmuring soothing love words, then, very gently, he mounted her and found his own completion. Curled beside him, her face pillowed on his shoulder, she was warm and snug, but her last thought before sleeping was, he's too good for me.

In the morning they ate toast and drank tea in bed, and read the newspapers that had plopped through the letterbox. Freya found it more than just pleasant, so nice to have an agreeable man about the place. They lunched in the pub down the road and walked in the park, then went back to the house and made love again, but when evening came and Monday loomed she turned to him and said,

'I'm away at the conference on Tuesday.'

He kept an arm around her, almost ready to leave. 'Damn it, I'd forgotten. The Continuous Professional Development bash, run on the British Heritage training budget.'

'I'm expected to attend, but keep me informed of what's going on.'

'Of course,' he promised, then grinned. 'It'll give me an excuse to ring you.'

'You don't need an excuse,' she assured him

'Devon, isn't it? When will you be back?'

'Saturday.'

'Nothing will get moving concerning the manor yet. You know how slowly these things grind.'

She welcomed the break, though had forgotten about it until reminded by Joan. She had been on other courses, but this was the first time she had attended such a prestigious one. When Andrew had gone she got through to Moira, trying the London flat. She caught her at home.

'Hello, darling. I'm in the bath. I'm frightfully busy

83

up here all next week. A film premiére to attend.. How did the dinner go?'

Freya filled in the details but omitted her nocturnal visitor, though did say, 'Andrew spent last night here with me.'

'Ah, and is he any good?' There was the slosh of water as Moira moved, and Freya heard her say, 'Oh, thank you, sweetie. Put it on the side. I'm on the phone to Freya.'

'Who have you got there?' Freya was amused yet exasperated. She had been hoping for some sensible advice.

'Giovanni.'

'What about his job?'

'He's working for me now. My bodyguard. He's really sweet . Has just brought me in a drink.'

'What happens when you get tired of him and move in someone new?'

'Don't pre-empt, darling. It may never happen. He suits me very well.'

'It will be a first if you stick with him.'

'What will be will be. Now, enough of me. You're off on this course? That's good. Get away from bothersome men and enjoy yourself. You may meet Mr Right. Anyway, have a time and ring me with all the gossip. 'Bye, pet.'

The course was being held at Holcombe Grange, just outside Exeter. It was a private college, but the students were on the Easter vacation and the house loaned out to organisations like that run by British Heritage. It was a rainy morning when Freya left home. A weekday, so the traffic wasn't a problem. She drove through the green, rolling Devonshire countryside, bypassed the city and followed her SatNav until the precise female voice led her to her destination. The rain had stopped and the sun had come out.

She was gazing, awestruck, at the frontage of this perfect example of mid-Victorian Gothic, when a lanky young man leaned in at her window and said, 'Are you here for the course, miss? Parking is round the back. Follow me.'

He was tanned and muscular, wearing a white shirt, khaki shorts and terrain sandals. His hair was long and tousled. She caught a whiff of the stables. Moira would fancy him, she decided, as he led her to where several other cars were parked. What is he, a kind of Mellors from Lady Loverley's Chatter?

He took her case from the boot. 'I'll carry that in for you.'

'Thanks. D'you work here?' She followed him to the reception area.

'Yep. It's usually full of teenagers from all over, paid for by rich parents.' He swung along and she had trouble keeping up with his stride, holding on to a bag containing a lap-top, and another with toiletries.

'Are they a pain?'

'Not really. I get on all right with them. Most are homesick, coming from China and I don't know where. I look after the horses and live above the stable. Riding is part of the curriculum. My name's Jason, by the way,'

'And mine is Freya...Freya Mullin.'

'Nice to meet you, Freya.' He smiled and she responded.

He could probably get along with almost anyone, she thought. In a way he reminded her of an older Danny, amiable and easygoing but not to be messed with. About twenty, perhaps? Maybe it was time she took Moira's advice and tried a younger man. Sexual attraction was a puzzle. The words of a 1930's song came back to her. *They're either to young or too old. They're either too green or too bold.*

She was welcomed by the couple who were running the event, an earnest middle-aged lady called Mary and a grey-haired lecturer who went by the name of Robert. There were other helpers in the background. Jason was given her room number and he disappeared with her case. Nothing could have been more civilised

She guessed this would be the ambience throughout the stay — civilised, scholarly, jolly and, as she complained to Moira down the phone, 'It's already boring the arse off me!' .

This was unfair, and she knew it. She had been given the opportunity to better her position and made up her mind to take full advantage of it.

Her room was on the second floor. It had a fine view over the garden and grounds and was pleasant and functional. She opened one of the drawers in the bedside cabinet and was surprised to find tampons, lubricant and a packet of condoms. Obviously, these belonged to the student who usually occupied it. This made her feel at home and she wondered about the girl, what she was studying and how many boyfriends she had. Did she spread it around or was she faithful to one?

Lunch was taken in the dining hall, where she sat at a one of the many round tables along with half-a-dozen others. The full contingent had not yet arrived, but she gathered that fifty were expected. It reminded her of the academy in the Harry Potter stories. Her companions were chatty and she was soon in possession of the relevant facts about their lives.

She introduced herself. 'I'm Freya Mullin. I work for British Heritage in Blackheath and district.' There was a polite ripple of interest but this sharpened as she added, 'We're about to investigate Daubeney Manor.'

'Gosh! Lucky old you!' commented Sylvia, a breezy woman of thirty plus. 'This has been on the cards for ages, hasn't it?'

'Supposed to be very old and important,' chipped in Bill, a lecturer and expert. He was wiry and thinning of hair. So far there was no one that roused a modicum of interest in Freya's loins, apart from Jason.

The pudding arrived, or cheese and biscuits, whichever one preferred. Freya chose the latter, reaching for the Stilton. 'It's been bought by Maxwell Sinclair and he wants to make alterations.'

'Not *the* Maxwell Sinclair?' Sylvia paused in lifting a spoonful of stewed apple and custard to her lips.

'The very one.' This gave Freya a warm feeling. She actually knew the great man. It might even be said that her knowledge of him was intimate.

'I saw him on BBC2 not long ago. My goodness, he is *so* clever!' Sylvia enthused. Several of Freya's other luncheon companions nodded and agreed. 'You've met him?'

'Oh, yes. Several times. In fact, I had dinner with him at the manor last Friday evening.'

That did it. She was suddenly in demand, everyone wanting to know details. She was a tad annoyed with herself for using Maxwell to edge her way in. It would have been more satisfying had she been taken to their hearts on her own merits.

It appeared that there were no trips planned for that day, giving everyone a chance to settle in. Tomorrow, they were to visit an ancient site near Dartmoor, using the college buses and drivers, and taking a packed lunch.

A roam around the house, a short rest, followed by dinner, then several of the more lively sparks suggested a trip to the local pub. It was in the nearby village, and they decided to share taxis. Freya showered and changed. Appearances had to be maintained, and she felt free and adventurous. It was stimulating to be with people interested in the same subjects as herself. Some of them might be fuddy-duddies, but on the whole they were fellow-enthusiasts., and this mitigated a whole heap of hidebound opinions.

The Kicking Donkey was one of those ale-houses steeped in history, found only in England. It had been established when, long ago, some enterprising housewife had hung a besom outside her door, indicating that she was open for the sale of ale and food and welcomed the weary traveller. Freya felt at home, and went up to the bar, ordering a gin and tonic. She wished she could smoke, but this had been banned. Her attention was drawn to a noisy group playing darts. Jason was the ringleader, handsome in a white vest that displayed his tanned arms, and tight, figure-hugging jeans . She was very aware of the substantial bulge behind the zip. Their eyes met and he grinned at her. A solitary hormone stirred in her groin. She turned her back on him, but possibilities ran through her mind. Don't be a bloody fool! she lectured herself and ordered another drink.

Several people from the course engaged her in conversation, and it was stimulating to talk with like-minded men and women who had one thing in common—the love of old, interesting buildings. But even as she exchanged opinions with them, her attention kept straying to Jason, embarrassed to find him staring back, open invitation in his eyes.

At one point, she excused herself from the group and made for the ladies toilet. There she stood looking at herself in the mirror as she dried her hands, resentful that life had forced her to be on her own again. It was much more comfortable to have a partner, no matter what kind of a bastard he turned out to be. Moira would have disagreed forcefully, but she was miles away. Freya knew she'd be attending the course alone even if still living with Carl. But at least he would have been someone to phone and go home to. It made her feel bleak.

When she stepped out into the corridor it was to find herself confronting Jason. He had just come through the door of the Gents. 'Hi, there,' he said, and braced his arms against the wall on either side, imprisoning her.

'Hello,' she answered nervously, knowing that she should be firm with him, but unable to do so. He smelled nice, of beer and deodorant and shower gel.

'I live over the stable. Why don't you drop in for a nightcap, when you get back?'

'I shall be too tired. Have an early start in the morning…'

'Bollocks!' This was the first time for hours that she had heard this expression. So far, everyone was on their best behaviour. Jason made her feel at ease.

His arms left the wall and closed around her. She was pressed against his chest, and she liked it. 'I don't know…' she temporised.

'Take a chance. Live a little.' His mouth hovered above hers and she wanted him to kiss her. At that moment a man entered the corridor and they sprang apart. Ignoring them, he went into the toilet.

She shook her head, though her heart was racing. 'I can't promise.'

'Catch you later.' Jason winked as he left her, very sure of himself.

Freya was thrown into a panic, one part of her wanting to take up his challenge, the other, more sensible bit urging her to go straight to bed when she returned to Holcombe Grange, and ignore him in future. But by the time she had had a couple more drinks and got back to base, the atmosphere of the beautiful moonlight night urged her to at least take a peek at Jason's stable dwelling. She found herself standing outside, and he was waiting for her.

'How did you know I'd be here?' She demanded.

'Don't talk. Come inside,' he whispered. The light was dim, the air hay-sweet, and horses rustled in their stalls, disturbed by visitors at that late hour. Jason spoke soothingly. 'It's all right, silly old darlings. No one is going to hurt you. Back to sleep now.'

'Is this the only entrance to your place?' Freya was unable to do other that go along with him.

'No, no. There's a door at the back, but I wanted you to see my sweethearts.' He leaned over one of the rails and she joined him, admiring the sleek black mare who tossed her head and whinnied, recognising him. When he passed on to another, the animal greeted him in the same way, obviously at ease.

'You've got the knack.' She commented.

'Animals and women. They're like putty in my hands,' he chuckled.

This could have sounded conceited but he had such a

way with him that she didn't take offence. Indeed, it somehow added to his attraction. With an arm around her waist he walked her to stairs that led to a landing. He opened a door, flicked a switch, and she followed him into a neat little flat 'This is cosy,' she said, while he held her close.

'It was a loft where the grooms slept, but some enterprising person had it transformed. It's OK. Suits me. It's private and I'm near the horses.'

'Do you entertain any of the students? 'Even as she asked him, she was telling herself that it was none of her business. This would never be anything but a one-night stand, maybe two.

His smile was disarming, his eyes honest. 'Some of the older ones. Believe me, most of them are up for it, experienced in fucking.'

His living room was combined with a fitted kitchen. 'Can I offer you a glass of cider?' He held the bottle in his hand, along with two glasses.

'No, thanks. I've had enough to drink tonight.'

'Then let me show you my bedroom.' He put down the bottle and laced her fingers lightly with his. 'The bathroom is over there, by the way.'

She stopped questioning her motives and the rights and wrongs of it, going with the flow. The bedroom was as neat as the rest of the flat. He seemed to take a pride in it. 'It's nice,' she murmured as he guided her towards the bed

'Take it easy, Freya, and you'd better call me Jason. This is not exactly the moment to be formal, is it? Sit down and part your legs a little. I want to try something that I think you'll like.'

She did as he suggested, raising her skirt. He lifted

it higher and went down between her knees, caressing her thighs and pushing aside her panties. Freya sat there as if turned to stone, but inside she was reduced to jelly. He certainly knew his business —gentle, admiring, using his fingers to comb through her pubic bush and find her epicentre. She looked into his handsome, boyish face and caressed his hair. Her clitoris was throbbing under his expert touch and she wanted more.

Now he used his free hand to unzip his jeans and take out his erection. 'I want you to see it,' he said.

She looked down It was presentable, as much as the male appendage ever is, dark-skinned, solid, with the foreskin retracted over a wet and shiny red helm. She didn't know what to say, then murmured, 'It's fine.'

'You like it?'

'I do.'

'You want it in you?'

Oh, God! Men and their cocks! she thought, while nodding and agreeing. They're so proud of that extra appendage! And it's not such a big deal after all. Aloud she said, 'What about a condom?'

'Aren't you on the pill?'

'Yes, but pregnancy isn't the issue.'

'You mean disease? I can assure you that I only go with clean girls.'

'How can you be sure? I've a condom in my bag.'

'All right, but not quite yet.'

Now, still kneeling, he raised himself and rested his weapon against her vulva, somewhat hampered by her knickers. He managed to insert it and she felt the pressure— hard, insistent, pushing inside her, but managing no more than the knob. He rested it there, lifting her crop-top and mouthing her nipples through the lacy bra.

The position was not very comfortable and she wanted to lie down and also make sure she was protected. Extricating herself, she took the condom out and stretched on the bed. It was a single, but big enough for their purpose. Taking this as an open invitation which, of course, it was, Jason lost no time in stripping off his clothes, displaying a muscular body. Freya was impressed, running her hands over all that beautifully tanned flesh and slipping the rubber over his large dick. He, in turn, started to undress her slowly, as if he was unwrapping a precious gift. This was more than just flattering, and she was being prepared every step of the way. Knowing this did not deter her from desiring him. In fact it increased her libido and she became impatient, but Jason wasn't to be hurried.

She was too excited to be astonished at his performance. That came afterwards. Now he had her naked and gazed at her with the greatest satisfaction He sat astride her, his cock bobbing against her belly, his hands on her breasts, than leaned down to capture her mouth. His tasted cider-sweet, his tongue mobile and firm. Her own answered his, tangling in a dance of desire. He slid down her body and that self-same tongue played with her clitoris, licking, arousing, until she could feel the indescribable sensation of orgasm rising and rising until it peaked. She cried out as she came, her whole body afire.

He withdrew softly and then pushed his penis into her, adding to the exquisite sensation as her inner muscles clamped round it, locking as he banged against her, all tenderness vanished. He was intent on finding his own release, mounting her almost brutally, and she loved every minute of it. Gasping and tearing at him, she wanted to own him, use him, make him her plaything, denying any other woman access to him. It was a madness that lasted for a moment only. Once he had grunted and thrust and come within her, this ridiculous obsession had disappeared.

As he rolled off her and flopped back, the condom looking slightly ridiculous and somewhat obscene on his rapidly deflating organ, Freya found herself wanting to gather up her scattered clothing and leave.

CHAPTER 6

Maxwell kept his secret close. Like a miser with his hoard, he held it to him, brooded over it, felt enormously clever and altogether superior to everyone else. He was reluctant to share it for the moment. Later, he might. It would bring him even more praise and fame, and this appealed to him, but not yet

For a day or two after his discovery, he hardly dared venture there, terrified that someone might follow him. On first finding it, he had carefully removed sufficient stone to enable him to squeeze through. Stepping within the shrine, for that is what he decided it must be, he had stood with a rapidly beating heart, shining the torch. Such treasures! Not so much their value in money, though this would be considerable, but because of their uniqueness. He lost touch with time, having no idea how long he was there. Afraid to disturb anything, he feasted his eyes on the wonders that filled the cave which, he assumed, had been hollowed out centuries before.

Roman? A cursory inspection suggested this, but he couldn't be sure as yet. He knew that he would have to reveal his find for carbon dating and further examination. But just for that space in time it was his and his alone and he had sat there, gloating over it. A place of worship? Undoubtedly. To the pagan god, Pan, by the look of it. He had goat's legs, horns and an enormous phallus. But the most significant find of all was a leather-bound journal and a letter. He opened both with trembling fingers, held the letter to the light and read:

"October 17th, in the year of Our Lord, 1799. Illness is upon me and I fear that I have but a short time to live. My son, James, will inherit, though I fear my fortunes are much reduced. However, I have garnered my remaining strength to seal up the shrine. The folly will remain in existence but not this. Dedicated to Pan many years ago by a person unknown. I have preserved it, making obeisance to him, and presenting him with offerings of virgin blood. Who knows? Perchance another lusty fellow may come upon it and continue in this worship. It is my sincere wish that he may obtain as much pleasure as myself, Lord Sebastian Bartram of Daubeney Manor."

Maxwell laid this down reverently. It was yellow with age and fragile. On opening the journal, he found it crammed with jottings, mostly describing orgies held in the folly and who attended them, with names of the maidens deflowered .There was much reading to be had there and he placed it in his pocket, along with the letter, then took himself off to his study, unable to believe his in credible luck.

All other considerations had been wiped from his mind, even Freya. Again and again he returned underground, taking measurements and photos, though hardly daring to expose it to light or possible bacteria. The journal intrigued him, and he felt a kinship with its writer. Lord Sebastian sounded as if he was a man after his own heart. At last, needing to share this discovery with someone, he phoned Jeff.

'I've come across something odd,' he began.

'Odd? How come?'

Jeff had been a friend and confidante for years but even so, Maxwell hesitated. 'Are you alone?'

'Sure. What's all this cloak and dagger stuff?'

'Lola's not there?'

'Nope. Come on, Max. Spill the beans.'

'I want you to come down right away. I've something to show you.'

'Now you've got me guessing. Give us a clue.'

'It's old and rare and bloody mysterious.'

'I'll be there pronto.'

'Don't bring Lola.'

'She won't like it.'

'Tough.'

Jeff arrived that evening. At once, Maxwell whisked him into the study. He had given Donna and Hilary the night off. Once inside he poured two snifters of whisky and handed Jeff the journal and letter. 'What do you make of these?'

Jeff took them in his hands. 'Phew! Where the hell did they come from?'

Maxwell gave a wry smile and shrugged his shoulders. 'Here. In the foundations of this house, would you believe? Left by a former owner, Lord Sebastian Bartram.'

'But I thought you'd already found a grotto beneath the folly.'

'I had a feeling there was more and approached it from this end. I found a shrine, Jeff, dedicated to Pan, and it seems that Lord Sebastian knew of it, too, and used it as the focal point for his parties, though never letting his followers into the secret. He dedicated innocent young girls to Pan in exchange for wealth and pleasure.'

Jeff laid the objects on the table, and sipped his whiskey. 'Doesn't look like Pan listened. The financial affairs were in ruins, apparently. What do you intend to do with it now? Will you tell the British Heritage people?'

Maxwell's jaw set stubbornly. 'I'd like to keep it for myself. We could have fun down there.'

Jeff ran a hand through his untidy red hair. 'You'd better let me see it.'

Maxwell almost refused. He was possessive, but there was no one he trusted more. Not so much Jeff's loyalty, but his need to share something so extraordinary that induce him to keep it to himself until the time was ripe.

'Come with me and prepare to be gob-smacked,' Maxwell said, and took him below.

Freya was enjoying an exhilarating sense of freedom. There was little time for idleness, a strict routine maintained. This included visits to sites and lectures illustrated by slides of important structures like centuries old farm-buildings and dwellings that had started life as hall-houses back in the thirteenth century. In those days there was a fire in the centre and a hole in the roof above it to carry away the smoke. Everyone lived, ate and slept there, including the animals.

She drank in every moment, coming to life, putting forward her expertise and talking as if she would never stop, and not bothering to contact Moira. The days were passing all too quickly. As for the nights? She spent part of each with Jason,

There was something incredibly sexy and sweet about a young lover. Stamina, too; he could come several times in quick succession. His skin was smooth and unwrinkled, having a light sprinkling of fuzz, thickening around the genitals. He was strong, muscular, and with hair to die for. Freya knew this to be a one-off. Most likely she wouldn't ever see him again once she had left Holcombe Grange. One thing was for sure; she'd never forget him.

'You'll be here tomorrow tonight?' he asked as the time for departure drew closer.

She snuggled up to him in the narrow bed, as naked as he was, thinking how lovely it would be if life consisted of kisses and caresses with someone as genuine as him. He smelled wholesome, of cleanliness and the spicy odour of come. Running her foot up his leg, she paused at his balls, toeing them gently.

'Try to keep me away. Of course, I'll be here. There's a farewell dinner at the Grange but I'll leave early, make the excuse of having to pack.'

'Will you give me your mobile number? I'd like us to keep in touch.' His cock was standing proud, roused into action again by the playful tickling of her big toe.

It was impossible to refuse him when his agile fingers started to roam around her clitoris. 'Later,' she gasped. 'Just carry on with what you're doing.'

She remembered this and their final encounter as she drove away from Devon on Saturday morning, heading for Blackheath. Her thoughts turned to Maxwell and Andrew. She had phoned him a couple of times, and learned that there was no development regarding Daubeney Manor. The paperwork was still grinding through the bureaucratic mills. Andrew was more concerned about telling her how much he was missing her. This was gratifying, but she wished she had an excuse to ring Maxwell Her pulse quickened at the thought of seeing him again soon. There was no reason why this should happen until Monday at the earliest.

She opened her front door, relieved to be home again. It smelled musty and she picked up the mail from the door mat, mostly junk, a couple of statements from her bank, and bills addressed to Carl. She tossed the latter on the hall-table, along with others, then went round opening windows. There were several messages on the answer-phone. One was from Andrew asking that she let him know when she arrived and another from Moira.

'Hi there, sweetie! I'm coming down at the weekend. Give me a bell and we'll meet up. Dying to hear about your adventures…filthy, I hope!'

Freya nearly dropped the receiver when she listened to the last message. 'Freya. Phone me. You are invited to afternoon tea at four o'clock on Sunday. Maxwell.'

Her heart leaped. Curiosity, anticipation, nervousness and, above all, desire, sped through her in quick succession. What could he want?

She declined Andrew's invitation to go out, pleading weariness, and did the same to Moira, then left Maxwell a message of acceptance. After this she shopped for essentials and went to bed early, indulging in watching Saturday night rubbish on the TV. Her hand slipped down between her thighs and she daydreamed of Jason as she masturbated before falling asleep.

'Come on, Jennie love. We've time for a quick one before getting tea ready.' James Armitage pushed her back against the kitchen table. They were alone; the other members of staff enjoying Sunday off.

She slapped him playfully. 'We can't. Behave yourself, Jim.'

He sighed and stood away, watching while she patted her hair and smoothed down her apron, then he asked. 'Who's he got coming this time? His mate has gone home, hasn't he?'

'Mr Plover? Oh, yes, but they were thick as thieves,

up to something, no doubt.'

'Isn't the boss always at it? That Lola! What a tart! She's got great tits!'

Jennie's mouth thinned and she threw him a warning glance. 'You keep your eyes off 'em! Aren't mine good enough for you?'

"Course they are. I'd prove it right now. If you'd let me.'

Her smile made her look like a girl, not the mother of a teenage son. 'Just you wait until we've finished here, then I'll show you what's what,' she promised.

He ran a hand under her skirt and familiarised himself with her rounded buttocks, before popping on his white gloves and continuing to prepare the tea-things; bone china cups, milk jug and sugar-basin, cakes on a silver stand, the tea-pot, also silver, and a little kettle placed over a heater. He bore these sedately into the drawing-room.

Freya was already seated there, having been greeted at the front door by Maxwell. Unsure of what to wear, finally deciding on something casual, she was relieved to find him dressed in jeans and a denim shirt, open at the neck, with thong sandals on bare feet. These made him appear less formidable. So did his welcoming smile.

'It's nice to see you again. Did you enjoy the conference?'

She was nonplussed. 'How did you know about that?'

'Andrew told me you were away for a few days.'

So, it was 'Andrew' now, was it? They were on Christian name terms. Aloud, she said, 'I had a most enlightening time.' She was referring to Jason, but couldn't tell him about that little indiscretion.

'Well done. I've attended such gatherings in my time,

and given lectures at them, too.' He cocked an eyebrow at the kettle singing away over the heater. 'Shall I be mother? Milk or lemon?'

'Milk, please.' She was contemplating how his presence must have stirred the scholarly ladies. She could imagine how the ones she had just left would have been in a great state of agitation and hero-worship, no matter how sensible they strove to be. He handed her a cup. 'Thank you.' she said.

He sat back in a deep armchair opposite her, and she was thrown by the keen scrutiny of his tiger eyes. He was not wearing glasses, and looked more than ever like a matinee idol. There was something so elegant and graceful about him. She found herself tongue-tied when she most wanted to be bright and intelligent and entertaining. He passed the plate of wafer-thin cucumber sandwiches.

'British Heritage is being long-winded. As you will understand, I'm keen to get everything settled and alterations made so that I can begin entertaining.'

Ah, is this why he invited me? she wondered, while replying, 'Sorry. There's nothing I can do to hurry them up.'

'I wasn't expecting you to. I wanted to see you. In fact, I've a feeling we could have a lot in common.' He oozed charm and, despite herself, she was falling under his spell again.

'I was impressed by your playing. I love music.'

'So do I.' He proffered the cake-stand. 'At one time it was a toss between going into archaeology or attending the Royal Academy and studying the piano seriously.'

'Do you regret not doing so?' This was better. Freya was losing some of her shyness.

A shadow passed over his face. 'It was my father's wish that I made something of myself in this field, not fritter away my time on a musical career.'

'He was ambitious for you?'

'Very much so.' The bitterness in his tone gave her a glimpse into his past. She found herself thinking that those who have been wounded are dangerous, for they know how to survive.

'You have a great gift.'

He shrugged this off. 'I don't practice enough.'

'That's a shame. I'd like to hear you play again.'

'Later, perhaps. We have business to discuss first.'

'Business?'

He smiled again, that slightly cynical smile. 'Not entirely business. I prefer to call it pleasure. Can I trust you?'

'I hope so.' She was becoming even more confused. 'Unless it contravenes the ethics of my contract.'

'Supposing I was offering to share a truly remarkable find with you, one that I wished to keep a secret for the time being? Would your job come first?'

She wished so much that he wouldn't look at her in that way. His eyes were mesmerising, her body answering his male attraction, and she desired nothing more than to promise him anything under the sun.

'You should know perfectly well that I can't betray my employers. Besides, there is my reputation to consider. I want to gain more qualifications and rise in my chosen field.' The words came out in a rush, and she feared she was expressing herself badly.

To make matters worse, he reached over and took her hand in his. His fingers were strong and warm, making her want to have them exploring the most intimate places of her body. 'Don't worry, Freya. This will enhance your reputation, when I decide to make it public.'

'What exactly is this mysterious something?' She tried to reply normally, while wishing she hadn't accepted his invitation to tea.

He answered her question with another, letting her hand drop. 'How much do you know about ancient religions?'

'Some, but buildings are my real interest.' She missed the warmth of his touch.

He proffered the cake-stand, saying, 'Jennie makes them.'

She waved it away. 'They look delicious, but no thanks.' How long was he going to keep up this game? The tension was mounting between them.

'More tea?'

'I should be going.' All this trivia when she wanted to ask him, Were you in my bedroom the night I stayed here?

He looked her in the eyes, as if reading this thought. 'Not yet, surely? I want to show you the folly.'

'I wasn't aware of one.'

'None of your people know about it. They haven't explored the outside yet. For the time being, this shall be our secret. Yes?'

Curiosity killed the cat, she mused, but was unable to refuse him.

The sun was setting and the manor resplendent in the golden glow of early evening. Maxwell offered her his arm and they strolled across the lawn to where trees hid a ruined building. At a glance Freya was able to date it as a Georgian mock temple, used by the aristocratic owners as a place of entertainment, wherein to hold picnics and evening parties. One of the noblemen must have visited

Europe and come back from Italy with ideas of architecture that he resolved to reproduce .in his garden.

'It's lovely,' she said, walking between columns that would have once upheld the domed roof. 'Are you going to have it restored?'

'I rather like it as it is. There's a kind of decadence about it, don't you agree? I'll bet there were some goings-on in the old days…young bucks betting and seducing, drinking and wenching. I sometimes regret not having been born then.'

'You'd have fitted in perfectly. The costume of the day would have suited you.'

'I'm thinking of holding a fancy-dress party when the work on the manor is near completion. Will you come, Freya, be the innocent maiden falling for the blandishments of the lord?'

The light was fading and she was all too aware of the over-the-top romantic atmosphere. Birds were settling to roost and bats skittered and squeaked as they circled the rooftop. The air was perfumed and she felt intoxicated by the presence of this man.

'I shall accept your invitation, if I'm still around.' She moved a little further away from him.

'Are you thinking of leaving?'

'I shall go where my work takes me.' And where fate leads me, her mind ran on. Would Andrew be a part of her future?

He seemed very remote as she stood there with Maxwell, whose personality was so powerful that he eclipsed other men. And yet she had a perfectly nice guy who would come rushing over if she picked up the phone. She wondered why women go for the bad boys — the wasters, alcoholics, drug addicts and womanisers. Hadn't she fallen for Carl and wasn't he of this ilk? Women felt challenged to reform the rake but, when they did so and he became a domesticated pussy-cat, they lost interest.

'Would you like to see more?' He indicated a slab, hidden by bushes.

'What else is there?'

'I'll show you, but keep it to yourself.' It was too tantalising to refuse and when she nodded, he shifted the slab, revelling an opening. Memories of the dungeon rushed into her mind, and she hesitated as he held out his hand. 'Come along. It's quite safe. There are steps.'

She peered down as he took his lighter to candles that stood on ledges. Now was the moment to retreat, but her sense of adventure urged her on. He had spoken the truth. The steps proved to be perfectly solid and, on reaching floor level, it was to find a large cavern, though hardly a natural structure. It had been designed and made by man. The folly hid this secret chamber where once, she guessed, the celebrations above had been repeated below, forming a grotto typical of the era when such entertainments had been the rage among the nobility. The walls glistened with semi-precious stones and paintings had been added, the subjects erotic. Gods and goddess fornicated in Grecian groves. Cupid was much in evidence, firing his arrows. There were centaurs and satyrs, with naked nymphs riding their enormous phalli.

'My God! This is priceless!' Freya gasped as Maxwell lit even more candles.

'I don't want it made public. It's my private pleasure ground. I shall only bring those I can trust here. I intend to make use of it as the former owners did'

'Surely you want to share it with the public?' She was sharply reminded of that first occasion when she had been alone with him underground, but this place was different, having an air of luxury and decadence.

'Not necessarily. That's why I'm asking you not to mention it to Andrew. I know that I can trust you.' He ran a hand down the side of her face, as gentle as a whisper. Then, his voice deepening and very seductive, he asked, 'Would you like to act out some of the delights that those libertines once practiced?'

'I don't know.' She did, of course, but was trying to deny her desire.

He spread his hands, indicating the décor, the dimness and the antiquity. . 'Do you like it?'

'It frightens, me.'

He smiled. 'Surely not? Let me blindfold you, blanking out light, and then allow your feelings, instincts, hidden urges to manifest,'

He whipped off her scarf and covered her eyes. She stiffened and tried to remove it, but he captured her hands. Deprived of sight and restrained by his iron grip, it seemed as if her other senses had sharpened. She could smell the candles and his after-shave, along with the scent of his hair. He pushed up her T-shirt, and she heard and felt the zipper of her jeans running down. Then he bore her back and back until hard stone chilled her bare spine. He stretched her arms out on either side, and there was a click as cuffs were fastened to her wrists and then attached to chains. She couldn't move.

'What are you doing, Maxwell?

For answer, he pulled her jeans down further and then the tiny thong. The air was cold on her pubis. 'I'm creating a perfect, lewd picture. You look good enough to eat, and certainly to fuck. Your skin glows against the dark wall, and your hair shines in the dimness. I love the sight of your blind eyes and the anxiety of your mouth, but above all are your eager nipples, straining towards me, begging for caresses.' And his fingers were on them, pinching, stroking, making them harden even more.

'Let me go!' The conventional side of her protested, but the other, earthy part wanted him to go on.

He didn't answer. It was as if he knew the animal longings within her. Now she felt his fingers on her clitoris, a rapid stroke that ran from the base to the tip, almost too hard, then diving into the wetness pooling at her vulva and spreading it up and over. She became unaware of the manacles chaffing her wrists and the ache in her arms. Her breathing was ragged. All she wanted was to have the burning between her legs satisfied. She could feel his erection pressing against her thigh and longed to have it within her, but he was deliberately denying her. He brought her close to orgasm, using his fingers and bending to caress her with his tongue, but each time she almost reached the peak, he withdrew, teasing and tormenting her.

'Not so fast, little one,' he chided, and slapped her across the tops of her bare legs. 'You have a lot to learn. The joys of pain and pleasure, for example. Like this,' and he struck her again, a forceful blow that made her cry out. He ignored her and subjected her to his hard palm again, once, twice, thrice.

'Stop it.' She was angry with him for hurting and frustrating her.

'You don't really mean that.' He moved to her breasts, sucking the nipples, while his hand cupped her mound, the middle finger tickling her clitoris. The burning in her thighs added to this sensation.

His penis was exposed, large and hard, nudging its way

into her wet sex. He thrust several times, while she strained against him, rejoicing in the feel of him inside her as she had wanted since first catching sight of him. On the verge of climax by his caresses, the glorious feeling of his invasion tipped her over the edge. She yelped as she came and he speeded up, deep within her as he sought his pleasure. She felt him climax, the hot charge of semen flooding her, and was thankful that she was on the pill, though conception was not the only danger.

He withdrew and released her. She took off the blindfold and adjusted her clothing, unable to look at him. Then, 'Have you brought anyone else here?' she asked.

'Lola.'

Her heart sank like a stone. 'I see. So I wasn't the first?'

'Does that make any difference?' he answered, with a quizzical lift if his eyebrows. 'What we did just now was entirely unique to us. Can't you see that?'

'And is this what you wanted to show me? The folly with its secret cave, that I mustn't mention to Andrew?'

'That's right.' He gripped her hand to help her mount the stairs, blowing out the candles as they went, then replacing the slab. It as full dark by now and he took her back to the house, then to the drawing-room. He pushed her into an armchair, poured her a brandy and one for himself. 'Sit there. I'll play for you.'

Freya leaned her head back against the cushion, glass in hand, wondering if she had dreamed the whole episode, but the wetness between her thighs was real enough. She had had intercourse with Maxwell Sinclair. Now he was seated at the piano, those hands that had chastised her and brought her to bliss now touching the keys. The room was softly lit and he knew the piece by heart, absorbed in it as he started to play *The Mephisto Waltz* by Franz Liszt. It was seductive, devilish, conjuring visions of Satan playing the violin while his naked acolytes whirled in mad dance around him.

Maxwell was strange, and she was beginning to accept this, becoming absorbed in his life-style, though terrified that she might be falling under the spell of obsessive love.

CHAPTER 7

Maxwell didn't suggest that Freya stay the night. She couldn't have done so anyway, as she had a work meeting with Andrew in the morning. She sobered up with black coffee and then drove herself home. He made no attempt to arrange another rendezvous. She had the uneasy feeling that, having added another notch to his bedpost, he was no longer interested.

She tossed and turned, unable to sleep, eventually going down and making a cup of tea, then carrying it back to bed along with the biscuit tin. No good for the figure, but that was the least of her problems. She regretted giving in to her desire .It had been intensely satisfying physically, but was emotionally charged. Every time she moved she could feel where Maxwell had slapped her, nd her wrists were sore from the manacles. Yet alongside the pain was a curious sensation of pleasure. Was this what he was trying to teach her?

When she dozed off at last, her dreams were hag-ridden and she still felt disoriented when the alarm woke her. How could she face Andrew? And how to keep her promise to Maxwell regarding the grotto beneath the folly?

Monday morning was usually a pain anyhow. Why did one have to earn a living? And yet, she concluded as she showered and got ready, without that framework of existence life would be aimless, with too much time on one's hands. Unless, of course, there was some great ambition or creative force that drove one to achieve the heights of music or writing or art. She had neither, apart from an interest in history and ancient buildings.

With Carl out of the picture, there was no longer anyone to share the day-to-day routine. She had enjoyed more lovers recently than ever before, but even this left a feeling of dissatisfaction. Where was her soul-mate? Was there such a thing?

She experienced a slight quiver of anticipation at seeing Andrew, but even then she felt guilty as hell regarding Jason and Maxwell. This angered her. It was none of his bloody business! Just because he had fucked her didn't mean that he owned her. She was pre-menstrual and crabby, ready to chew the carpet, yet glad of these symptoms. Had she conceived during the past weeks, she wouldn't have a clue whose sperm had reached its goal. Now she understood the phrase, "It's a wise child who knows its own father."

Fortunately she was off bounds sexually for the next few days. Also British Heritage had given its consent to Maxwell's alterations and the team set about the work involved. One bright spot in all this was the return of her old friend, Grant Foster. Down-to-earth and practical, he was like a ray of sunshine

He arrived one morning clad in dungarees and a baseball cap. 'Hi, there,' he said, dumping down his bag of tools. 'How're tricks?'

'OK.' She was pleased to see him. Here was someone who knew the business inside out. She could talk to him about the manor in a down-to-earth way, with no sentimentality and flim-flam or Maxwell's territorial attitude.

He sat on the stairs and got out his flask. 'Coffee?'

'Thanks.' She slipped into the space beside him. It was early and there was no one else about, not even Hilary and Donna.

'What have you been doing with yourself?' He unearthed a packet of biscuits.

'Oh, this and that. I went to a conference type thing.'

'Interesting?'

'Some of it.' She thought of Jason.

He nodded and glanced around the Great Hall. 'I'll bet this place is a rabbit-warren. Priest-holes and all sorts. I can't wait to explore, starting in the attics.'

'I've been up there. The roof needs attention.' It was very pleasant sitting there talking shop with someone who knew the ropes. She wondered how it was that they hadn't kept in touch.

She watched his hands dispensing more coffee into plastic mugs. They were well-shaped, tanned and strong. His shoulders were wide under the white tee-shirt and the denim dungarees fitted him well, but loose enough for comfort and crawling around in narrow spaces as his work demanded. She had a lot more in common with him than Andrew or Maxwell. Andrew was needy, and as for Maxwell? He was a law unto himself and difficult to fathom.

'Where are you living?'

'I bought a house in Bristol. It's in Clifton.'

'A nice area. Near the university.' She wanted to know more about his personal life. Did he have a girl-friend? She found it hard to believe that he didn't, not an attractive, intelligent man like him.

'I'm away on jobs quite a lot, though work is slowing because of the recession everywhere.'

She grimaced. 'I know. It's even hitting the sale of old buildings. People are sticking where they are at present.' She wanted to continue talking with him, but he stood up, stretching widely.

'Time I went exploring. If I'm not back by dark, send out a search party. I may have been kidnapped by the Wicked Witch of the West.'

Freya smiled back but Lola Descartes sprang to mind. Had she been successful in seducing him after the dinner party? She hoped not, surprised by the jealousy that stabbed her.

Moira was concerned about Freya Her father's last words as he lay dying in hospital after the crash were, 'Look out for her, Moira.' Heartbroken, she had promised. Many men had made love to her since, but no one had taken his place.

Waking in her London flat, with the luscious Giovanna sprawled naked beside her, Freya had been on her mind. She reached for the phone. It was eleven in the morning but she caught her on her mobile. 'Darling, how are you?'

'I'm fine. What's wrong?'

'I think you need a break. Why not come up for the weekend?'

'I suppose I could.' Freya sounded doubtful.

'Have you anything planned?'

'Not really.'

Moira caught something in her voice that was worrying. 'Everything all right?' she asked. Giovanni stirred and captured her with one thigh, his swollen cock diverting her. 'Down, boy,' she muttered.

Freya assured her, saying, 'Of course everything's all right. We're busy at the manor.'

'That's what I mean. You're over-doing it. Come to London and we'll have a crack.' Moira managed to concentrate while being caressed by Giovanni. 'How about next weekend?'

She could almost hear Freya's brain buzzing as she sought excuses not to come. Was she so eager to continue this stalemate with her men? 'That sounds fine,' she said, after a pause.

'Make it Friday afternoon and we can hit the town that night, as well as Saturday after we've shopped until we drop. I've an important party to attend. It's at Lola Descartes' place. You've met her, haven't you? Well, I've a write-up to do for *Hot Life*. She says it's cool to bring you along, and my faithful bodyguard, too.' Moira's attention was being channelled to him. He knew the way to her heart, via her clitoris.

Freya agreed and hung up. Moira turned and drew her lover into her arms, sighing contentedly. He really was ideal, and, apparently, besotted by her. This might even be the one, she thought dreamily, then told herself not to be daft. How many times before had she felt like this, only to be let down? Enjoy it to the full while it's there and not look into the future, she decided, and whaled in with relish.

Freya had visited Moira's pent-house apartment before. Not often, because Carl and her friend never bothered to hide their antipathy and were constantly sniping at one another. He was obviously envious of her lifestyle and her influence over Freya. This was the first time she had been there alone and was freshly impressed by the way old warehouses situated by the side of the River Thames had been turned into prestigious living areas. Top-of-the-range and exclusive, they were inhabited by executives and celebrities. She left her car in the underground parking lot, knowing it would be safe. Maximum security was in operation throughout the entire complex.

She took the lift to Moira's eerie at the top of the building, wondering what was in store. She admitted that she needed a break, both from the rigorous work involved with the manor, but also from her own confused emotions. She was curious to learn more about Lola, one of Maxwell's intimates. Maybe through her she could begin to fathom this baffling individual.

'Come in, darling.' Moira was at the door. She is wearing a towelling robe and her hair was wet. 'I'm getting in a spot of sunbathing.'

'Is it warm enough?' Freya plonked down her overnight bag and followed her through the hall and into the kitchen. Spacious and airy, the apartment had everything, even a roof-garden with a pool.

'It's Ok, for this time of year. Let's take our coffee up there.' She made Instant as she talked, neat and quick in her movements, and soon Freya was following her into the open air.

The first thing she saw was Giovanni lying on a lounger, stripped to a jock-strap. It outlined his package and his olive skin was already darkening in the sunshine. It was idyllic, and Freya's loneliness stabbed like a knife in the heart. Moira may not intend this to be a full-term relationship, but just for the moment she had a man.

He raised a lazy hand, greeting Freya and saying , 'Welcome to London.'

She could feel the stresses and strains of Blackheath falling away. She occupied another lounger with a big striped parasol fixed above it, shading her eyes and face but not her arms and legs. She stretched out and lifted her skirt, feeling those blessed rays caressing her bare skin. This was the life. She was glad that she was there.

Moira and Giovanni took her out later. They phoned for a taxi. It was much less hassle than using one's own vehicle what with parking problems and the ban on drinking and driving, to say nothing of vandalism and outright car-knapping. Freya found herself whisked through the West End traffic to a small, extremely exclusive club in Soho, where Moira was instantly recognised by bar-staff and clients.

It was sophisticated and far removed from Charlie's establishment. Somewhat intimidated, Freya could find little to say, introduced to this person and that. She didn't begin to loosen up until she had downed a few drinks, putting an alcoholic haze between her and them. Later Moira told her that she made quite a hit, but she couldn't remember much about it.

She wanted to sleep as soon as her head hit the pillow, but was too aware of Giovanni exuberantly fucking Moira in a nearby room 'Bugger,' she sighed 'I feel like joining them. Three in a bed. I've never tried it but wouldn't mind having a go.' She got up and staggered into the hall, then paused, but only for an instant. The sounds were too enticing. She opened the bedroom door.

She stood there dumbstruck. She had never seen a couple in the throes of sexual congress, not even in a porn movie. Clive had been into these but she had always made an excuse for not watching, embarrassed by finding such intimate moments reduced to prostitution to satisfy the greedy film industry. What she now saw changed her mind. He was stretched on his back and she was bending over, giving him head.

They were a beautiful couple, in their prime. Moira's body was firm but shapely and Giovanna's like that of a male model. Every woman's dream of a handsome lover. There was nothing salacious or crude about the way they were enjoying one another, and Freya found it intensely arousing.

Moira took her mouth away from his crotch, looked up, smiled and said, 'There you are, darling. Come over here.'

She lay with him in her king-sized bed, and both were naked. Freya realised that she, too, was nude. She couldn't recall undressing. Mesmerized, she approached slowly. Moira stretched out an arm and gentle pulled her down. Freya resisted for an instant 'But this is so odd. You were my father's girl-friend.'

Moira gave a throaty chuckle. 'And he asked me to take care of you. I'm doing just that.'

Giovanna was looking at them as if Christmas had arrived early. Moira caressed Freya's breasts and they responded, the nipples crimping, hard and needy.

She sank back among the pillows, inhaling the scent of Moira's juices. It resembled her own, like fresh sea-shells, so different from that of the male. I'm in bed with a woman, she thought, in no way alarmed. I never dreamed I would do this, but it's fine. I feel safe, and confident of being satisfied.

Moira turned on her side and hugged Freya close, pressing her mound against her. The sensation was strange but exciting. Freya could feel her clitoris responding, and ground herself against a cunt for the first time ever. Moira's pubis was covered with dark hair, neatly trimmed to form a bikini line, so soft to touch. The sight and feel of it aroused Freya beyond imagining. It no longer mattered who did it, just as long as she was brought to orgasm.

Giovanni took advantage of Moira's position, nestled against her back and inserted his cock into her vagina. Freya could feel his movements as he thrust in and out. It diverted her attention from her own mounting climax and she felt bereft when Moira laughed and got on all fours, accepting him and, at the same time, manipulating Freya's clitoris with one hand.

Freya was aware of the rhythm of his thrusting and could hear his moans as he tried to resist coming. He pulled out for a moment, and cupped Moira's cleft, working on her clit as she leaned over and sucked Freya's.

'Ooh! Ah! Go on! Don't stop!' Freya begged, pleasure swamping her as she reached her zenith. She came back to earth to catch Moira's cries as she, too, was brought to climax by Giovanni's skilful fingers.

Then, 'My turn,' he said and shifted position to lie between Freya's legs and guide his engorged cock into her slippery wet sex. He was big and she clenched her inner muscles around that long, thick organ, her contractions still rippling through her. She looked up into Moira's eyes, hoping that she didn't mind her lover servicing another woman, but she simply smiled and nodded and whispered, 'Enjoy, pet, and I shall enjoy watching.'

Giovanni gave a final, massive thrust and yelled his pleasure, spunk released into the condom. Then he lightly kissed Freya's cheek, withdrew, removed the rubber, flung his arms round Moira and bore her back on to the mattress with him, expressing his delight in a spate of romantic-sounding Italian, as if forgetting Freya's part in it.

She slept in their bed and showered with them in the morning, all shyness gone. True to her word, Moira arranged a shopping trip and Giovanni went along to carry the plastic bags printed with the names of prestigious stores. Despite the credit squeeze, these seemed to be busy, women strolling through the magnificent emporiums, spending money on clothes as if there was no tomorrow. Freya was circumspect. She liked bargains and often patronised the local charity shops, especially those in rich areas where clothes were discarded after one season.

'Go on. Treat yourself,' Moira urged, half in, half out of the changing room where Freya was trying on a dress.

It was sexy and glamorous and for a fleeting second she imagined donning it for Maxwell. Then commonsense reasserted itself and she shook her head and started to take it off. 'When should I wear such a thing?'

Moira expressed disappointment. 'You're always so practical. Rather like your father. He was a rock star but had his head screwed on the right way. He never squandered money either. Finished here? The restaurant is something, I can tell you. It's the done thing to do, although a cup of tea costs an arm and a leg, and as for a slice of their famous chocolate cake! Don't even think about it.'

Visiting Moira was like riding on a switch-back. She was full of boundless energy, and Freya wanted a nap when they got back, but there was no time and she was swept into the flurry of getting ready to attend Lola's bash. She almost regretted not buying the dress, but made the most of the one she had packed. Aware of butterflies in the stomach, she answered Moira's call and left for the party.

Moira's eyes were gimlet sharp as Lola headed towards them. 'Don't even think about it,' she hissed, her hand tightening on Giovanni's arm. 'Last night was OK. Something that I wanted to do, but Lola Descartes is another bucket of kippers.'

He grinned and shrugged, saying, 'I don't understand. What is this "bucket of kippers?"'

'A figure of speech, darling. Don't worry about it. Just keep your cock in your trousers where she's concerned.'

Freya caught their conversation and it confirmed what she had already gleaned concerning Lola. Her residence was impressive, a mansion near Hyde Park worth millions. Gossip had it that this had been purchased for her by a politician high in the Government. No one really knew and though the paparazzi worried at the story like a scavengers with a bone, nothing had been brought to life.

Moira had filled Freya in with all this, and she stood in reception marvelling at the gorgeous architecture and way in which the décor had been carefully preserved. This interested her more than the crowd who made up Lola's guests. She recognised some of them from media coverage and Moira was in her element, waving to this person and that, drawing others into conversation, making mental notes of items that might titillate her readers.

Music boomed, a nervy, edgy sound. and Freya gathered it was the latest recording from an up and coming band, *Blurb Rap*, whose lead singer had recently appeared on a Big Brother show. Known as Jay, he was present, a savage looking young man, wearing dread-locks and a snarl. Lola was hovering in attendance, treating him like a resurrected Jesus Christ. Moira informed Freya that in her opinion he was a conceited, talentless twat who had struck lucky by getting on the telly. Whatever, he was the flavour of the month.

There was food and drink in abundance and nothing could have been more decorous. Then, as time passed, the guests thinned out and the newshounds took themselves off. A bevy of shaven-headed, evening-suited bouncers stood on guard at the doors. Moira had not yet been able to corner Lola, but now seized the chance.

'Can I ask you a few questions?' she began, while Lola draped herself elegantly on a damask covered settee, cocktail glass in one hand.

'Of course. I know you from somewhere, don't I?'

Moira was noncommittal. 'We've seen each other around.'

'And don't I recognise the woman with you?'

'Freya Mullin? She's a friend of mine. You said she could come along.'

'Ah, now I remember. She was at Maxwell Sinclair's for dinner. To do with British Heritage.'

'You've got it in one. Now, would you care to tell me about your latest project?' Moira got out her pen and notebook. 'I want an exclusive. *Hot Life* are paying a fortune.'

'I know. My agent has told me about it. Why else d'you think I'd be wasting my time? By the way, I don't want the slightest reference to anything you may see here later. If you should be so foolish, then I shall sue, and make fucking sure that you never work again. No paper or magazine will dare employ you.'

Her tone was arrogant and insulting and Moira marked

her card, thinking, I don't much care for you, lady. We'll see who comes out on top.

Freya and Giovanni had left her to it, and he escorted her like a perfect gentleman, making certain that she had a drink and didn't feel left isolated. It was hard to believe that he had entered her body last night, his attitude towards her brotherly, making no reference to the incident. When Moira finished with Lola and came to find them, she was boiling with rage.

'That patronising bitch! I'll get her one day! God, you'd have been proud of me. I didn't lose it, and my calm spiked her guns. I got what I wanted from her and she's asked us to stay on, if we like. I think it might be interesting.'

More drinks were served and the remaining guests adjourned to the second floor of the building and into the games and exercise rooms. They joined others already there, plus masseurs and trainers, all part of Lola's team who kept her in trim. There was a sauna, a hot tub and a swimming pool. Also various pieces of equipment for toning the muscles, although some were being used for another purpose, or so it seemed to Freya's inexperienced eye. She recognised manacles similar to those Maxwell had fastened to her, and a contraption over which a woman was stretched, her naked rump upraised to receive the paddle a man was brandishing.

'What the hell are they up to?' She paused, catching Moira by the arm.

'Looks like an S and M party. My, my …I suspected that Lola was into this.'

'Do we have to join in?' Playing strange games with Max was all very well, but Freya had no desire to try it with strangers.

'I gather it's up to us, though I'll make sure I stick with Giovanni. He's quite handy with the whip and punishes me when I'm in the mood.' She took his hand and guided him to where a row of flails, canes and floggers hung.

Left alone, Freya lurked in the background until Lola approached her. 'Won't you have fun with us? I'm sure Maxwell would approve.'

Before she knew what was happening she found herself in the hot tub, stripped to her thong. The water bubbled about her as she sat there. It was pleasant, though embarrassing to be sharing it with four others, all naked, the men sporting fully fledged erections and the woman languid and ready for any kind of sexual attention. There were fingers everywhere, and she felt them on her body, male hands, female hands, and smiling faces and the cheerful, stirring heat seeking out her most private places. It all seemed so casual and almost normal, yet even so she wanted to leave, but was prevented by one of the men.

'Oh, come on. Let's have some fun! No one is shy here. Your first time? You'll learn to love it. Here, grab hold of my prick, and have a feel of Polly's tits.'

'Thank you, but no. I've got to go!' she stammered and shook off the restraining hands, nearly slipping on the wet tiles in her hurry to escape. She swathed herself in a towel and found her clothes, seeking a cubicle in which to dress.

She drew back the curtain of the first she came to, and then stopped. Two men were in the most intimate of embraces. The younger was bent over, hands on his cock, while the older, heavier of the pair grunted as he propelled his penis into the other's rectum. Too immersed in their mutual pleasure, they did not acknowledge Freya's presence and she backed out, mortified.

Dear God, was there no end to this? Apparently not, for everywhere men and women were fucking. Not only that, men were enjoying men and women caressing members of their own sex. The surroundings were great, the atmosphere relaxing and they could use the paraphernalia for its original purpose if they chose, but most of them were indulging their own personal tastes. And no one more so than Lola, who was screwing the balls off the rock-star, Jay.

Freya crept into a corner and struggled into her clothes, hoping no one would see her and try to drag her into the fray. Did Maxwell know of Lola's inclinations? No doubt he did, and it occurred to her that maybe he, too, was into it. She couldn't see Moira, and wondered if she was indulging somewhere with Giovanni. She hadn't appeared to be shocked or surprised. It seemed that Freya was the odd one out and she wanted to leave, find a cab and go back to Moira's apartment. This wasn't her scene.

Or so she thought.

Suddenly, two men materialised beside her. One was blond and the other dark. They were wearing tee-shirts and shorts. 'Hello there!' the dark one said. 'I'm Greg.'

'And I'm Phil,' put in the blond.

'Are you guests?'

'We're Lola's trainers. We keep her in shape, and tonight we're on loan to anyone who fancies us. Do you?' Greg gave her a wicked grin. They both reminded her of Jason.

'I'm just going.'

'Oh, no! You can't. It's only just starting to swing!' they chorused.

She found herself being propelled towards a massage couch and, despite her protests, lifted on to it. The slippery black leather was covered by a large white towel. Greg persuaded her out of her dress and underwear.

Phil rolled her over so that she lay on her stomach, covering her with another towel from the waist down. Why was she submitting to them? she wondered, while waiting to see what they were going to do next.

At first it was nothing alarming. They anointed her skin with perfumed oil and both used their skills to massage her, strong hands finding and relieving all those little aches. She was very aware of them standing, on either side of her, their crotches at eye level. Phil kneaded her upper arms and shoulders, while Greg worked on her lower spine and thighs. His hand slipped between her legs, and she shivered as he touched her crack. It was almost as if by accident. His breathing became deeper, and she watched his groin. The bulge in his shorts was more noticeable, so close to her that one small movement would bring it into contact with her flesh.

A crowd had gathered, interested spectators making comments while indulging in their own pleasures. The men sported erections and the women were as randy as bitches on heat. Freya had gone too far down this strange road to feel embarrassed. Her trainers kept other hands away from her, concentrating on their job, but gradually their attentions became more intimate, especially after they had moved her to lie on her back. The small towel was removed. She was stripped for all to see, her breasts and pubis on display.

'Are you going to shag her?' asked Lola, elbowing her way to the front with Jay in tow. He was looking decidedly crumpled. Too much cocaine and too much adult sex.

He couldn't handle it, reverting to his very ordinary background. She flicked at him with a riding whip and he looked bewildered.

'Would you like to see us do it?' Greg asked, grinning widely. 'Your wish is our command, lady.'

She nodded, and her smile was malicious. Freya was struck by the thought that maybe she resented the attention Maxwell had paid her. She protested as Phil dropped his shorts and positioned himself so that his cock was pressed against her face. He held her head and she couldn't move away. She tasted his pre-come on her lips and tried to keep her mouth closed but he was forceful, all gentleness banished, a man driven by the urge to release his spunk.

Greg, wearing a condom on his prick, was standing at the foot of the couch. He lifted Freya's legs and placed an ankle on each of his shoulders. Lola urged him on and flourished her whip, catching him across the back. Her friends cheered. Freya fought to escape his large organ, but in so doing she opened her mouth to protest. Phil took advantage of this, plunging his rubber-clad weapon between her lips. She tried to close her teeth, but he held her jaw, his helm pressing against the back of her throat, making her gag.

Greg rubbered up and his lubricated cock found its goal, impaling her. She was under attack in two areas and gaining no pleasure from either. Pain and humiliation were her only sensations and she wanted to scream for Moira but Phil's phallus made this impossible. She didn't like the taste of the condom, or the smell of him or his utter selfishness. She was crushed by Greg's weight, overwhelmed by his rampant desire, made to feel worthless by these two men who, in the beginning, she had thought to be friendly.

They took their time, performing for Lola, and she laughed and encouraged them, wrapping her thigh around Jay and rubbing her pubis against him. The guests seemed inspired by the show, masturbating or chasing each other, falling to the floor and copulating. It was a crazy saturnalia, fuelled by alcohol and drugs and lust.

Freya managed to bite Phil's cock and, 'Bitch!' he shouted, pulling back.

'For God's sake finish!' she yelled at Greg, her nails becoming talons as she clawed at his back .

'Ignore her!' Lola commanded, her whip descending to flick Freya wherever she could.

Greg continued to thrust, sweat running down his face, and Lola thrashed him repeatedly. Freya closed her eyes, willing the ordeal to be over, tormented by his usage of her and the smart of the lash.

Suddenly everything stopped. There was dead silence. Then she heard someone say, 'What the hell's going on here?'

She looked up into Maxwell's furious face.

CHAPTER 8

It was like a hurricane hitting the room. Maxwell's rage focused on Lola. He snatched up the whip and used it on her viciously. Phil and Greg retreated to a safe distance. The crowd stared. Freya slid from the couch, wrapping the towel around her.

Moira appeared with Giovanni. 'What's wrong?' she shouted above Lola's howls.

Freya threw herself into her arms. 'Get me out of here.'

'Sorry to have left you, pet, but I didn't realise that she had it in for you.'

Lola prostrated herself at Maxwell's feet, but he turned on Moira. 'Why did you bring Freya?'

'I didn't realise that it would be like this. I'm a journalist and I came to interview Miss Descartes. Freya is my guest for the weekend and was asked along.'

'I thought it would please you, Max,' Lola had stopped sobbing and was gazing up at him, all wide-eyed admiration.

He shook her off. 'You thought wrong. I had nearly decided not to accept your invitation. Just as well that I did. You know that Freya is working at the manor with her colleges. Have you no discretion?'

Seeing that there wasn't about to be an entertaining full-scale row, the audience had gone back to their pleasures. Moira helped Freya into her clothes and wrapped a poncho around her, saying, 'We'll leave now. Thank you for the interview, Miss Descartes,' and she rang a taxi on her mobile.

When they had gone, Lola rubbed herself round Maxwell's legs like a pedigree cat in season. They were alone momentarily. 'Didn't I do well, master?' she whispered.

He stared down at her, scowling darkly. Although this episode had been engineered between them, he hadn't realised how much it would infuriate him when he actually saw Freya being used by Phil and Greg. His anger had exploded, and it was genuine.

Lola had told him that Freya would be at the party with Moira, and they had come up with the plan to see how far she would go. He had arranged to arrive late and take it from there. His own reaction had astonished him. The few remaining shreds of decency that remained within him had rebelled. He regretted agreeing to the conniving Lola's scheme. He knew she was a spiteful vixen, but useful in many respects.

For some obscure reason Freya intrigued him. He was finding it hard to break through her reserve. Even whipping and fucking her hadn't had the desired effect of turning her into his slave. She was just too independent and it baffled him. He shrugged this off temporarily and turned his attention to the guests. Several important people were present, and he was never one to turn up the opportunity for blackmail, if not in hard cash then in favours bartered for his silence.

He could have had any of the women, but selected his confederate, Lola. He pulled her to her feet by her hair, ripped off what remained of her clothes, and spread her, face down, over the massage couch, arms stretched above her head and wrists tied. She moaned and wailed, not in fear but in anticipation. Maxwell threw off his jacket and rolled up his shirt-sleeves, baring his brown, sinewy arms. A short, multi-tailed flogger was substituted for the whip. He eyed Lola's shoulders and back, then swiped across them. She shuddered, lying limply, and he paid attention to her buttocks. It took several blows before the skin started to redden.

Maxwell could do just as he wished with this willing submissive. He fulfilled his need to punish her for his disappointment in Freya. Then, as he watched that lissom body helpless before his will, his cock became erect. He threw the flogger away, opened his trousers and let his serpent have its way. It was already prepared, sheathed in black rubber. Lola wailed as, standing between her legs, he drove it into her anus. The tightness proved pain and pleasure combined, easing as he persisted. He fed his lust with images of Freya as he used Lola brutally though, judging by her noises, she was enjoying it.

Next time, he promised himself as his climax surged, next time it will be Freya.

'Well, I'll be buggered! Fancy him turning up!' Moira said as she unlocked the door of her apartment.

Freya shook her head, unable to speak. She sank on to the couch while Giovanni asked, 'Who is this so angry man and why does everyone take shit from him?'

Moira flopped down beside Freya, kicked off her shoes, stretched out her legs and rested her feet on the coffee table. 'I don't think you want to know, darling. He's Freya's client, at the moment, or rather that of British Heritage. They are getting to work on alterations to his manor house near Blackheath.'

'Then why did he go to this party?' He came round to stand behind her, his hands massaging her shoulders. She rested back and closed her eyes in ecstasy. 'Oh, yes, yes! You do that so well.'

'That's what I'd like to know,' put in Freya, skin

stinging from Lola's crop, pussy wet and sore from enforced intercourse.

'And I'm going to discover answers. Leave it to me. I'll use my reporter's nose to ferret out the truth. I'm knackered and ready for bed. Don't worry about it, Freya. I'm certain there's some rational explanation, but I'll hazard a guess that those two are closer than you thought.'

Freya couldn't rest until she had showered, but though she succeeded in washing off the touch of her two unwelcome lovers, there was no way she could remove the memory of Maxwell's behaviour from her mind. Moira seemed to be unfazed. In fact, by the sounds coming from her bedroom, she and Giovanni had found it sexually stimulating. Freya envied them and ducked her head under the pillow, seeking sleep.

'Did you enjoy your weekend away?' Andrew was in his office when Freya reported there on Monday morning.

'It was fine. I did some shopping, then went to a party with Moira where she interviewed Lola Descartes. Moira's a journalist, you know.'

'You've told me about her. And I met Lola at Sinclair's.'

I'm going on too much because I feel guilty, she thought. But what have I got to hide? It's really nothing to do with him. She changed the subject to work. They had several points to discuss and the meeting was almost formal, except when he touched her bottom in passing and looked at her with twinkling eyes.

'Grant is making a condition report. There's a lot to be done and I'd better get over there.' She was uneasy and wanted to leave.

He walked her to the door. 'Can we meet up for a drink tonight?'

It was more difficult to think of an excuse than to accept, so she nodded. He kissed her cheek, so wholesome and straightforward a person that she cursed herself for wilfully preferring the wild one.

Later in the day she had her head in the wide chimney in the manor's kitchen, examining a bread-oven that had come to light. She ducked back, startled when Grant spoke to her . 'Hello, Freya. How're tricks? '

'Pretty good.' She dusted herself down, removing a smattering of soot. 'This place keeps on throwing up surprises, doesn't it?'

'I thought I'd tackle part of the grounds, as a change from The Hammer House of Horror in the roof. The folly, to be precise.'

This brought her up short. 'Maxwell has told you about that?'

'He doesn't keep interesting items from me. Would you like to examine it, too?'

'I've been there once, with him.' There seemed to be no need for secrecy now, but Max wanted it kept quiet, didn't he? Or maybe just the grotto? 'What does he intend to do about it with regard to historic records?'

Grant followed her into the rear garden and across the lawn towards the trees. 'It's Maxwell's property and he can do what he likes, now he's gained permission for alterations. Jeff Plover is his architect and I'm the surveyor and he pays for our services. If we find anything weird and wonderful we talk it over with him, and we keep shtoom if he doesn't want it spread around.'

Freya was familiar with these regulations, but nine times out of ten an owner would be proud to have any find on his land shared with the local museum, and certainly getting the Heritage people involved. Maxwell was different, and she could well believe he would keep hold of what he considered rightfully his.

'What about the conservation officer?' She suggested, uneasy with all this cloak and dagger stuff.

'*What* about him?'

'Won't he expect a detailed report?'

'Maybe. It's down to Maxwell. Come on. I want to explore the folly.'

She put on a bold front and gave Grant no hint of the intimacy that had taken place between her and Max on her former visit. The folly was at its picturesque best — ancient, sun-drenched, backed by woodland. She was very aware of Grant, and being there alone with this strapping, enthusiastic, handsome man— and old friend, to boot. He was lost to anything but his enthusiasm for the site.

'It needs to be stablised. I'm sure nothing has been done to it for years and that pillar over there looks as if it might collapse.' He paced around quickly, making notes. 'It's a lovely spot. Can't you imagine how it might be on a warm summer evening? Great for informal parties.'

Have you any idea how informal? she thought, still reeling from Lola's gathering. Maybe Grant was in on it, too. How friendly was he with Max? Were they all on his payroll? The idea was unpleasant, and yet she wondered if this was not engendered by her own feelings for the man. Did she want to be a part of his intimate circle?

'Ah,' Grant exclaimed, dropping to his knees close to the half hidden slab. 'What have we here? Maxwell said there might be a few surprises. He likes to keep me guessing.' It was a matter of moments before he had shifted the heavy stone and was peering down into the darkness. He looked back over his shoulder at Freya. 'Did you know about this?'

So what? She thought, on the edge of defiance. 'I did, as a matter of fact. He showed it to me not long ago. I didn't make a report as he particularly asked me not to, and I was respecting client confidentiality.'

'You've been down there?' He was already disappearing into the aperture.

'I have.' It was impossible not to remember every moment of that former descent. She lingered at the top. 'I'll stay here. I don't need to see it again.'

'It's up to you.' She could see the flash of his torch and heard him give a low whistle, followed by, 'Blimey! This is something else!' His voice sounded hollow and fainter as he moved further in. She heard him tapping walls, followed by silence as he noted down details, then reappeared. 'What a place! I expect you noticed that it has been kept in good order.'

'His doing, I guess.' She didn't know what else to say, memories crowding in.

'You've not mentioned it to anyone else? Andrew, for example? Maxwell told me not to discuss unusual objects I might unearth.'

'He's your boss, in effect.' This annoyed her and he went down a peg in her estimation, prepared to accept money for his silence.

'True. And the owner of the place, don't forget. Under no obligation to talk about anything he wants to keep to himself.'

'Most people would be excited and want to share it,' she grumbled, and started to walk back to the house.

He caught up with her, seemingly unaware of her feelings and she had to admit that on any other occasion she would not have been trouble. It was all to do with Maxwell, and it made her distinctly uncomfortable. She was rapidly going off Grant, glad when he left her to join Jeff. Did *he* also know of the grotto?

Feeling decidedly disgruntled, she plodded into the house, intending to knobble Donna and have her accompany her upstairs to inspect the linen-cupboards and built-in wardrobes. She pulled up short when she heard a piano. The drawing-room door was ajar and her heart skipped a beat as powerful chords reverberated into the Great Hall. She knew the piece. One of Chopin's *Preludes*, gloomy and moody, full of dazzling arpeggios and dire forebodings. The Polish genius was a consumptive and died young. Was he somehow aware of his fate as he composed this?

Maxwell was so absorbed in the music that he seemed unaware as she entered, drawn like steel to magnet by this masterful interpretation. He looked so different, almost possessed by the notes wrought by his flying fingers. She could hardly believe it was the same man who had bound and blindfolded her. Which was the real Maxwell? She stood, transfixed, with a crazy dream of reforming him in her mind. Good sense prevailed, and she turned to withdraw. There was no way she could take on such a task and he'd probably hate her for it. Concentrate on Andrew, she told herself. Forget Maxwell. Once this job is over you'll probably never see him again. Thank God!

The music stopped in mid flow, and she heard him say, 'Come over here, Freya.'

How long had he known she was there? It was uncanny.

She hesitated, then walked across the floor. 'I can't stop. I have work to get on with.'

He patted the piano stool beside him. 'Sit down.'

She obeyed. It seemed churlish to refuse, but mostly she didn't want him to know that she feared what he could do to her peace of mind. What had happened to her so far was bad enough. His left shoulder was firm against hers, his left thigh warm and strong. He moved his hands over the keys, summoning a dreamy melody.

'Debussy's *Clare de Lune*,' she murmured

He nodded, but didn't look at her. '*Moonlight*. So evocative. I can almost smell the fragrance of a warm summer's night and see a lake reflecting the silver trail.'

'Oh, yes,' she breathed, tears smarting behind her lids.

The music stopped and he turned on her, his mood changing in the blink of an eye. 'What were you doing with those two men?'

'Where? When?' His aggression frightened yet infuriated her.

'You know damn well! The other night, at Lola's orgy.'

He's mad! she thought, and tried to pull away. 'It was pretty obvious, wasn't it? I had been persuaded to join in the fun.'

'Willingly? Unwillingly?'

'What difference does it make to you? I'm a free agent.' She yanked at her arm and broke free, standing up. He pushed back the stool and dragged her between his thighs. Her hands came up, fingers like claws, ready to tear at his face.

'No, you don't!' He blocked her attack and held her there.

She was seething with rage. 'Let me go!' she demanded. 'This is ridiculous. Someone may come in at any moment, your lap-dog Hillary or the oh-so devoted Donna.'

'D'you think I'd care? Why are you fighting me? It seems like it's not so much me you fear, but yourself.'

Shit! She thought, while it was still possible to marshal her wits. Why did I wear a skirt today instead of sensible trousers? This makes it all too easy for him. Even as she stood there in the circle of his arms, she could feel herself yielding. She was pressed against his groin and her skirt was riding up and up, revealing her bare thighs with him between them. He eased forward and now she could feel his erection.

'Don't,' she pleaded, but he unzipped with one hand and she could feel the heat of him, unable to resist as he eased his cock against her.

Now he raised her legs, one by one, so that she was sitting on the stool, embracing him with her thighs. Her panties proved little obstacle and he dragged the crotch to one side, out of the way. Then she felt the pressure of his helm seeking entrance. She had enough sense left to be aware that it was bare. She struggled, but it was so hard to resist.

'What's wrong?' He stopped pushing, frowning at her resistance.

'You're not wearing a condom.'

'Dear God! Is that all? Here, put one on for me,' and he fished in an inner pocket and drew out a pack.

'Ha! Were you in the Boy Scouts and your motto is still "Be Prepared?"' Her sarcasm hid her hurt. Did he ever pass up the opportunity for a quick bonk? She had been turning hot for him, but this was like a dash of cold water.

'You're a prickly bitch, aren't you?' He growled, then

proceeded to rub his cock over her crack. 'All right, then. No penetrative sex, but how about this? Let me enjoy the outside of your lovely wet minge.'

It was too much to refuse, as he guided his cock to her labia, caressing the wings and concentrating on her clitoris. She sat with her thighs across his legs, open to him and all the pleasure such an experienced seducer could devise, cock head and fingers arousing her, his own pleasure matching hers. She arched her back and let the delight course through her, so aware of that magnificent organ being used as a tool for her satisfaction. Her bottom landed on the keys, producing an inharmonious, though rhythmical, sound. She hardly heard it. Waves of pleasure were rolling through her, gathering momentum and she sobbed as her orgasm reached its peak, dimly aware that he, too, was climaxing.

She sank down, her arms clinging to his neck, juices soaking into her skirt. She wanted to say something incredible foolish, like 'I love you,' but had enough sense to lock the words inside her. For once, he seemed to be lost, silently pulling away and fastening up. She stood, rearranging her wet knickers, managing to mumble, 'And where does this leave us?'

'Where indeed?' He seemed unusually distracted, and she was too embarrassed to press the point.

'I'm not usually so easy,' she blurted.

'Oh, no? What about the men at the party?'

'That isn't my style. I'd never been to anything like it before. It's not my scene. I'd had a bit too much to drink. I certainly didn't expect to see you there.'

'And what did you feel when you saw me?' It was as if he was coldly analysing her emotions.

'Shock. Surprise.'

'Not shame because your master had arrived and found you fucking two men?'

'Look, you're not my master.' Passion had been replaced with indignation. 'No one is my master, never has and never will be.'

He chuckled and lightly produced notes from the piano. 'Who are you trying to convince? Yourself?'

'Oh, you're impossible!' She snatched up her file and purse, then headed for the door, followed by his mocking laughter.

She was unsettled for the rest of the day, avoiding Grant, brusque with Donna, making notes about the age of the linen press and armoires but lacking her usual enthusiasm She left early, driving home and flopping on her bed, thoroughly disgruntled. She was annoyed with herself for falling so easily into Maxwell's trap. He only had to sit at the piano and she was lured like a rabbit towards a stoat. Never again! She vowed. I'm seeing Andrew tonight and shall endeavour to forget Max.

She picked up the cordless phone and dialled Moira. 'Hello. Can we talk?'

'Sure. I was about to ring you anyway. I've been finding out things about Lola and Maxwell.' She sounded breathy and excited.

'Go on. Dish the dirt.' Freya wasn't quite certain if she wanted to hear it or not, but Moira was launched.

'Well, I've been doing a bit of digging and unearthed quite a lot about our Lola and the enigmatic Maxwell.'

'Where from?' Freya sat up, leaning forward eagerly, the phone clamped to her ear.

'I have my sources. Seems like they run a secluded private club. This is how Max wants to use the manor, holding orgies and having influential but naughty people to stay. This puts him in a strong position, and Lola, too. Neither of them are above using blackmail, so I hear.'

'Can't they be stopped?'

'No one grasses on them. They know too much , besides those who use their services enjoy it, and don't want to give it up. We're talking about every perversion here, apart from those that include children and animals. Even they draw the line somewhere.'

'I see.' Freya felt soiled. Any romantic feelings engendered by the musical interlude earlier on now seemed tarnished. 'And Lola's party that we went to?'

'I think you were invited on purpose. She knew he would turn up. Be careful, Freya. He's a force to be reckoned with when he wants his own way.'

'I realise that.'

'Oh, Lord, you haven't, have you?'

Freya couldn't keep it from her. 'Yes, I have. This afternoon at the manor. He was playing the piano, and he's so talented. I tried to deny him, but I couldn't, and it means nothing to him …nothing at all.'

She wanted to cry, and Moira's sympathy made it worse. 'Keep away from him. Make sure you're never alone with the sod. What's happening with Andrew?'

'I'm meeting him tonight.'

'Good. Shag him to death! Get Maxwell out of your system. He's not worth it. Promise me!'

'I can't do that, not promise, I mean. He's just too strong for me, but I will encourage Andrew. Maybe I can fall for him after all. Thanks, Moira. I'll ring you later.'

She's right, Freya thought as she got up, stripped and had a shower. The warm cascade eased her, mind and body. Swivelling round, she could see her buttocks in the mirror tiles. There were faint marks left by Lola's crop. The sight of these sent a stab of longing through her, and she was both ashamed of her feelings and excited by them. What sort of a monster was she becoming if she was roused by the remembrance of being abuse? Not Lola's blows, but Maxwell's earlier ones. She indulged herself, reliving the episode by the piano. She could still smell him and feel his cock rubbing against her cleft, and reproduced the sensation with her fingers, so aroused that she reached a mind-blowing climax.

I'm going crazy, she thought as she came down, leaning against the shower wall and trembling. Pull yourself together, girl!

She did so, stepping out and using the bath towel rigorously, then applying her energy to dressing and make-up. Every time Maxwell appeared in her mind , she firmly blanked him and substituted Andrew. This became easier after a while and by the time she was ready to leave, she was certain that she'd got the matter under control.

Chapter 9

The pub was busy, and Andrew attentive. He had called for Freya around eight, suggesting that he drive, then she could have a drink. She needed one after the day she'd just had, but liked to be independent. However, if the worst came to the worst, she could always ring the cab office.

They didn't go to *Charlie's*. Andrew preferred something old-fashioned and *The Hunter's Moon* filled the bill. Several hundred years old, it was a typical English ale-house, and they were soon ensconced on an oak settle close to the fireplace. Although it was spring, logs smouldered between the andirons. Andrew drank orange-juice and Freya ordered a gin and tonic. She wanted a cigarette, but smoking was banned and she didn't much fancy going outside to a special area where tobacco addicts could indulge their habit.

'You're quiet. Is everything all right?' Andrew asked, amidst the buzz of convivial conversation around them

He was just too perceptive. 'Why shouldn't it be?' She twirled her glass between her fingers.

'Things going well at the manor?'

'Yes.' She squashed the urge to mention the grotto, telling herself that this was Grant's responsibility, not hers

'I shall inspect progress this week.' He clasped her free hand in his. 'I wanted to ask you something. It will be the Easter holiday soon, and I was wondering if you'd like to come away with me. I own a villa in Spain, near Seville, and it's a great time of the year, with fiestas and the first bull-fights on Easter Sunday. There's singing and flamenco and colourful processions.'

She didn't know what to say. She loved Spain and had been there on several occasions, but Andrew was asking her to go as his lover, not just a travelling companion. He was kind and handsome and a gentleman, but she feared to commit herself.

'I know it. Used to visit with my father when he did gigs there.'

'Or we could try Italy. There are excellent packages for opera fans. We could stay in Florence and do the Puccini Festival, visiting his birthplace, Lucca, then Torre Del Lago where he had a house by the lake and composed most of his masterpieces. It's kept as a museum, just as he left it. In nineteen-sixty, an open-air theatre was built for his works alone and they are staged every summer.'

She had to admit that the prospect thrilled her. 'I've heard of it and always wanted to go, but it sounds expensive.'

'Don't worry about that. My treat. You'll come?' He looked so boyishly eager that she hated to disappoint him, besides —why not? She had nothing else planned.

'Yes,' she said, borne on impulse and unhappiness and a second glass of gin.

'That's great. I'll find out about booking.'

He ordered pub food and everything was as good as it could get, given her muddled feelings, and when they left and he took her home, she couldn't do other than invite him in. It was late and he made no demands on her. She longed to sleep but knew that he wanted to screw her, though with Andrew it was always a case of 'making love'.

She complied, but more from a sense of duty than desire. He did all the right things, pressed the right buttons and her body responded to his touch on her clitoris. She came and it was good, then she fell asleep in his arms, and everything was fine until the return of morning light and sobriety.

He stirred when she did, waking fully and reluctant to let her go. She wriggled free, saying, 'Work It's seven-thirty. I'm meeting Grant at nine.'

She escaped into the shower, the spray invigorating, and the scent of gel pungent in her nostrils. She closed her eyes and allowed the jets to run over her body, seeking out her intimate places. The curtains parted and a naked Andrew joined her.

'I've almost finished.' She stepped aside.

'Not yet, surely?' His arms came round her wet body and the water cascaded over them.

It reminded her of the early days of her relationship with Carl. New lovers, they had often shared the shower. She closed her eyes and leaned back against Andrew's chest, feeling the firm cock pressing between her buttocks. He paused suddenly and she looked over her shoulder. 'What's wrong?'

'Where did you get those bruises?'

Oh, damn, she thought, saying quickly,' It must have been when I was scrambling through small spaces in the attics.'

He seemed satisfied with this, too absorbed in penetration and quickly reached his goal. Freya let him take his pleasure, not in the mood to climax herself, and when he had finished and was washing vigorously, she escaped. 'I really must dash. I'll ring you later.'

'Come and take a gander at this.' Grant was looking down on her from the trapdoor leading to part of the roof space.

Freya took a grip on the ladder and started to climb. He grabbed her wrist and hauled her up beside him. The torchlight showed thick dust, cobwebs and something else that immediately caught her attention. 'Arched beams,' she exclaimed, standing to see better.

'My guess is that this was once the ceiling, maybe that of an early hall, and floors have been added below it since. What do you think?'

'It looks very much like it. Smoke blackened in places as if a central fireplace once existed.' Freya was so engrossed that she forgot Andrew and Maxwell. It was good to get back to her roots.

'So when do you think this was built?' He was directing the torch beam upwards, sweeping the light over the rafters.

'The foundations? Probably in the thirteen hundreds, when all activity took place in the large room in the middle. This was added to as time went by. That's why it is such a mixture of styles, finishing up during the eighteenth century, when it was given a Palladian exterior and the folly was added.'

He grinned and gave a slow hand-clap. 'Well done, Miss Mullin You've got it in a nut-shell'

She could feel herself flushing. 'There no need to be sarcastic.'

He pulled a straight face. 'I'm not, I assure you. I admire your expertise, I swear it.'

She remembered university days when he had teased her unmercifully. They had always had this part-admiring, part-scornful relationship, and even now she couldn't tell if he was being serious. 'Shall you make a report to your boss?' she asked tartly.

He lowered the torch and sent its light skimming over

the rest of the large space. 'Maxwell? I guess so. He wants to know everything.'

'Have you discussed the grotto with him?'

'Sure. We went down there together and he told me that he'd done the refurbishment, though leaving most of the things as they were. He's delighted with it.'

'Will he tell Andrew?'

'I've no idea. My job is to see that everything isn't about to collapse.' Suddenly the torch was shining in her face, blinding her, and he was standing closer, saying,' What's the matter? You always were stand-offish at uni, and time hasn't improved this. Do you find me a right pain in the arse?'

She pushed the torch aside. 'It's not that. I'm just a bit surprised to find that you're so much under Maxwell's thumb. I wouldn't have thought you could be bought.'

'I find that insulting.' He sounded angry. 'I'm paid to do a job, and that's all there is to it.'

She was well aware that she was up there alone with him. This seemed to be becoming a habit with her; dark places and blokes! Either underground or high up. I shall be glad when I finished with Daubeney Manor, she vowed.

'I'll write a report on this,' she said. Making for the exit, she lowered herself through until her foot contacted the top rung of the ladder.

He was there above her. 'D'you need a hand?'

'No, thanks. I've been in more awkward places than this.' She wanted to get away from him, from everyone, free to think her own thoughts in peace.

She found a secluded corner of the garden. It was quiet, a sunny terrace where she opened her pack of sandwiches and poured coffee from her flask. She wished she had on a skirt instead of jeans, then she could have bared her legs to the warm rays, but when she thought about the roof she had just examined she was glad that she hadn't. She got out her pad and started to note down aspects of Grant's new discovery, but found it very hard to concentrate. Maybe Andrew was right and she *did a* need holiday away from it all. His offer had been more than generous, but her reaction was lukewarm.

Perhaps I'll take a break on my own, she thought, or go with Moira, though I guess she'd want to bring Giovanni along. Oh dear, sex and hormones are such a drag. I shall be almost glad when I'm too old for this malarkey.

It was then that she heard splashing and laughter from the swimming pool area. She thought she recognised Max's voice. Ignore it, she told herself, but found it quite impossible. Instead, she downed the coffee and repacked her bag, then walked round the house in the direction of the sounds. Turning a corner she came directly upon the pool. Max was there, wearing the briefest of trunks and looking for all the world like a Greek god. He wasn't alone. Lola was displaying herself in a miniscule bikini, her breasts bare and her beautiful body stretched out on a lounger. Jeff Plover was immersed in the pool. Lola spotted Freya immediately, lifting her sun-glasses from her nose and saying, 'We have company, Max.'

At once Freya felt herself coming under the scrutiny of his tigerish eyes. 'Freya, what a pleasant surprise. Won't you join us?'

'Thank you, but no. This is my lunch break and I should be returning to work. Your house requires a good deal of examination,' she managed to say in what she hoped was a professional manner.

'Oh, come along. What if I give my permission?' His smile was beguiling, and her doubts about him seemed so much nonsense.

'I don't work for you, but for British Heritage,' she reminded, hanging on to her sanity.

'I'm sure that august body wouldn't grudge you a swim on such a lovely day.'

He succeeded in making her feel like a novice instead of a respected member of her team. 'I don't have a costume with me,' she demurred.

'No problem. There are several in the changing rooms.' He indicated a row of chalets situated to one side.

Freya found herself in a hole. She could either refuse and look like a spineless idiot or agree and risk coming under his spell again. *But surely I've enough gumption to resist him?* She lectured herself. *After all, he's inviting me to use his swimming pool, nothing else.* He was challenging her, without a doubt, daring her to do it. And in front of that Lola creature, too. *Right,* she thought, *here goes!*

'I suppose I could spare half an hour,' she said and walked towards one of the chalets.

It was sparse but clean and she found a bikini to fit in one of the lockers. She stripped rapidly and slipped into the leopard-printed bottom. It was extremely brief, barely covering her pubes, and she adjusted the ties each side. The bra consisted of two cup, also attached by thongs, one forming a halter neck, the other fastening centre back.

Damn, she thought, giving a twirl in the long mirror. *I'm so white! Unlike Lola who has obviously spent time being sprayed in some expensive beauty salon.*

She pinned up her hair, snatched a towel from a rail and squared her shoulders, before stepping forth.

She was greeted by a wolf whistle. 'Wow!' Maxwell exclaimed. 'Why are you hiding your light under a bushel? You should be a model.'

Too embarrassed to reply, Freya made for the pool's edge, dropped the towel and immersed herself. She had hardly registered that the water was heated when Maxwell dived in, surfacing beside her. He tossed the hair back from his eyes. 'Is it warm enough for you? I keep it at a moderate temperature until the summer comes.'

'It's fine.' She made to swim away from him but he placed his hands each side of her waist and pulled her closer. Firm, tanned, well-muscled flesh pressed against her. It was hard to think straight in that intimate embrace, and she remembered her earlier immersion with Andrew. It had been nothing like as stirring as this.

Jeff swam up to them. A podgy man who grinned and raised his sandy brows. 'Is there room for a little one?'

'I wouldn't call it that little. Let me check it.' Lola slipped into the water. She made a grab for his crotch.

Max didn't move, just held Freya tightly and his companions laughed and groped each other and the atmosphere was tense with raw, uninhibited sex. It was infectious and every one of Freya's scruples was fading away. She could pretend that she and Max were in some private Garden of Eden, the only couple in the world and that he loved her and she was his mate.

He reached round and untied the bikini top, then pulled it so that it hung there, supported by the halter, her breasts bare, and the nipples peaking. At once his fingers found them, gently pinching, producing the most wonderful sensations. Next he released the ties at her hips and the thong fell away, floating in the water. He had bared his penis, apart from the transparent rubber that protected it. Before she had time to think or protest he had lifted her from her feet and inserted it between her thighs. They parted almost of their own volition and he was inside her, penetrating deeply while she gasped and clung to him. It was a fiery sensation, but she didn't come for there was no contact with her clitoris. He did, however, an unstoppable force sweeping him away.

His frantic plunging stopped, and he held her closely, the water lapping around them, the sun shining on their faces. Not far away, Jeff and Lola were reaching their own noisy climaxes, but even this didn't spoil the peace that enwrapped Freya. All right, so Maxwell had used her for his own selfish pleasure, but even this was of no odds. She felt so good in his arms. It seemed right, as if she had been born for this.

Then Grant suddenly appeared at the pool side, and his face was almost comical in its shock and disbelief. 'What the hell…?' he began, one glance showing him the scene. He recovered quickly, but the look he gave Freya burned like a brand.

She pulled away from Maxwell and fumbled for her bikini top, dragged it round to hide her breasts, and then managed to retrieve the tanga. Lola was nothing like as concerned, flaunting herself and shouting, 'Hi there! Come and join us! The more the merrier.'

'Not now. I'm working. I was looking for you, Freya. I've found some dates carved into one of the beams that we were examining earlier. But it seems like I'm interrupting something.' He turned to leave, but Freya was anxious that he didn't go off with a bad impression of her.

'Wait a moment,' she shouted and, finding the marble

steps, left the pool and wrapped the towel around her. 'I'll dress and come with you. Wait for me,' and she made a dash for the changing-rooms.

Grant was the very last person she would have wished to find her in such a compromising position. He was a working colleague and, as such, she valued his respect. To be discovered by him cavorting with, nay even worse, *fucking* a client was totally infra dig, and she was hugely embarrassed, wishing the ground would open and swallow her up.

She couldn't stop to dry herself properly and pulled on her clothes, leaving the bikini hanging on a hook, then forced herself to go out and face them all, Grant in particular. It was horrible. But she managed to say goodbye to Maxwell and the other two, almost as if nothing extraordinary had taken place, and marched off around the corner with Grant in tow.

'Sorry to have spoilt your fun,' he muttered. 'But I thought this was important and had no idea you'd be screwing our boss.'

'Is that what he is…our boss?' She temporised, putting off the inevitable question.

'In a manner of speaking …yes.'

'Wrong. He may pay your wages but he doesn't pay mine. I'm employed by British Heritage.'

'Stop slitting hairs. Anyway, it's bugger all to do with me.'

'Dead right it isn't. Now, can we get on?'

Once inside, he paused at the ladder leading to the roof, turning to her and saying, 'A word of warning. Maxwell's a player. You'd be wise not to get seriously involved with him. '

'Oh, so you know him personally do you? Have seen

him in action?' She feared this to be true but wasn't going to give him the satisfaction.

'Not exactly, but people talk.'

'I never listen to gossip,' she pronounced loftily and began to climb the ladder.

He came up behind, then when they stood under the beamed roof, caught her by the arm and hauled her closer, shouting, 'You are the most goddamn stubborn female I've ever met. OK, let him use and abuse you, but don't come running to me when it all goes pear-shaped.'

She shook him off. 'Get lost! You're the very last person on earth I'd ever ask for help!'

They worked in stony silence, although the date carved into the wood was exciting, giving them an accurate reading of the age of that part of the manor. Freya went home in a bad mood, furious with Max for tempting her again, and angry with Grant for catching them at it. She felt that she had lost face with him. There might not have been much love lost between them, but at least he had respected her. Now he would think her as much of a trollop as Lola. But sitting in her kitchen with a cup of tea and thinking it over, she had to confess that it was her own weakness where Max was concerned that angered her most of all.

She was disturbed by the phone and flew to it, heart soaring as she imagined it might be him. It was Andrew saying cheerfully, 'Italy's booked and we'll fly the weekend before Easter. We can get time off.'

Her feral self was disappointed because it was him, not Max, but her civilised being succeeded in sounding delighted. 'How lovely! I shall look forward to that tremendously,' while inside she was thinking, Dear God! Can I do it?

'Is that Freya Mullin?' It was a youthful male voice speaking to her on the mobile.

'Yes,' she answered, and then recognised him. 'Jason. This is a surprise.'

'I'm glad I found you Wasn't sure if I had your number right. Are you coming down to Exeter soon?'

She hadn't given it a thought, but now the prospect was pleasing. To see him again, so straightforward and uncomplicated. All he was interested in was a night or two of sex. 'Maybe,' she said, and turned down the telly with the remote, then perched on the arm of chair to continue this unexpected conversation.

'Oh, come on. What about next weekend? There's a decent motel not far away from here. I'd really like to see you again.'

'No regular girlfriend yet?' She found herself wanting to be in his company.

'Nothing worth mentioning. The talent on offer isn't a patch on you.'

A standard compliment, but it pleased her. 'Next weekend? It's a bit short notice but I think I can make it.' The notion of running away from her present suitors was enticing. A trip to Devon in the spring, shaking the dust of the manor from her feet and pretending to be someone else, just for a while. It was too tempting to refuse.

'Great! Shall I meet you at the Studland Motel on Friday evening? It's well marked on the map. I've a few days off and we can visit the coast on Saturday, if you like. You've got my number, haven't you, if anything crops up and you can't make it?'

'Yes, I have, and no, I don't think there's much to prevent me.'

'I can't wait. You're one hell of a sexy lady.'

'I'd have thought you would have forgotten all about me by now.'

'Christ no! It wasn't that long ago and I was right pissed off when you left.'

'I'll be with you on Friday,' she promised and he said goodbye and switched off, reluctantly, she thought.

Well, here's a turn-up for the books, she mused. It had brightened up her evening far more than Andrew's call. He had wanted her to go out with him, but she had made the excuse of having an early night. She felt a bit mean, for the trip to Florence would be wonderful and visiting the home of her favourite composer was thing she had always dreamed of, but all this was marred by his obvious expectations of her reaction to him. What would she do if he asked her to marry him? Had she been a settling down type of woman, it would have been ideal, but there was no way she was in love with him or wanted to be a domesticated wife and mother, although the idea of children appealed to her.

She allowed herself to anticipate a pleasant time with Jason and slept better than she had for a while. Next morning, in the office, she told Andrew that she would be away for the following weekend. The nimble lies sprang to her tongue. 'I'm going to Exeter to visit a fellow historian I met on the course at Holcombe Grange. She has kept in touch and invited me down.'

'Oh, that's nice for you, but I must admit I had hoped we could spend some time together, discussing the holiday, perhaps. We shall be seeing *Tosca* on the Friday night and *Turandot* on Saturday.'

'Wonderful,' she exclaimed and she meant it.

'Why don't we meet up tonight at my place and I'll

put on the DVD of one or the other, whichever you fancy?'

'Lovely,' she replied. 'I'll be there.'

The days passed and Freya succeeded in getting through them somehow. She avoided Grant and Maxwell, sheltering under the umbrella of Andrew's attention. She spent the evenings with him, listening to music, scanning brochures of the proposed trip and discussing Italy. More than that, they shared a bed, either at her place or his and it was all very cosy. She tried not to think about her proposed betrayal with Jason. It occurred to her that she was turning into a Jezebel or a slag or both.

'I shall miss you,' he said, when she set off late Friday afternoon.

'It's only as couple of days.' She kissed him warmly, feeling guilty and sorry and wishing she was a better person.

Her lack of feeling was emphasised when she crossed the Devon border with a light heart, looking forward to the escapade with Jason. The countryside was beautiful, the trees turning green and blossom starting to show. The birds were engaged in frenetic nest-building. The traffic was thinning by the time she reached Exeter and turned off towards Holcombe Grange. The motel was a discrete distance away. They were hardly likely to be spotted. She pulled up outside the modern, rather impersonal building and there was Jason, large as life and twice as natural. Her heart did a crazy summersault in her chest. She had almost forgotten how handsome he was.

He guided her to the parking lot and, when she got out, swept her into a bear-hug. 'It's so fucking good to see you! D'you want to eat or shall we go to our room? It's already booked.' The car-park was busy. Other people were using the convenient facilities of this stopping place.

'I wouldn't mind a cup of coffee.' He was obviously eager to get her knickers off, but it had been a hard day at work and a long drive. 'And then I need shower…'

'And then?' He kept an arm around her.

'We'll see,' she teased, although there wasn't the slightest doubt in her mind. It was going to be a heavy night of shagging.

He carried her bag and they signed in at the reception desk and picked up the keys of their room. It was equipped with a 'fridge and tea and coffee making paraphernalia and was neat and impersonal, as such places tend to be, complete with a king-sized bed. He tried to propel her towards it. 'Never mind about the shower, I love the smell of you. Get undressed.'

This was too much. If anyone was going to be in control then it must be her. 'I want a drink first.' She switched on the kettle and got out the makings. 'Would you like one?'

'All right.' He looked positively sulky.

This was gratifying and she realised that maybe it was fun to be the dominatrix. She'd never practiced this role before. There's a first time for everything, she decided, and sipped her coffee in a leisurely fashion. Let him wait until *she* decided that the time for action had come.

'Take your clothes off,' she commanded.

Jason expressed surprise, then grinned rather sheepishly. 'Your wish is my command, lady.'

'Good boy. I'm glad you've realised that.' She sat on the side of the bed and watched him as he stripped to his boxer shorts. He hesitated, and she added. 'Those, too.'

The sight of him naked was a severe test of her self

control. This specimen of lovely young manhood was hers to do with as she liked. And she *did* like, most definitely. His erect penis was bobbing as he approached her. 'I've dreamed of this moment.'

'When you were wanking, or with other girls?' She was determined to torment him,

'There hasn't been anyone since you.' He handled his tool, moving the foreskin back towards the shaft, the dome crimson with wanting.

'So you've masturbated and thought about me?' This gave her an enormous feeling of power.

'That's right. At least once a day. But you're here now and can't we go to bed?'

Freya stood up and took off her jacket then, very slowly, unbuttoned her blouse. Jason stood there transfixed, his hand caressing his cock with greater urgency. With all the skill of a striptease artist, Freya unzipped her skirt and let it drop. Her legs were bare and she stepped out of her shoes. Next she reached round and unclipped her bra but didn't let him see her breasts, keeping her back towards him. She heard him groan and quickened her pace. The last thing she wanted was for him to come off in his hand. She turned slowly, facing him, wearing nothing but her black lace thong.

'Lie down,' she ordered. He was ready to do anything she asked and made a lunge for her, but she stepped aside. 'Not yet. I want you on your back, arms stretched above your head, and you'll call me mistress'.

'OK, mistress. Whatever you want, but we didn't do anything like this before.'

'No questions. Do as you're told.'

When he was in position, watching half amused, half apprehensive, his cock standing as straight as a poker, she picked up her scarf and fastened his right wrist to the bed-post. 'What are you doing?' He was laughing, but puzzled.

'We playing slaves and mistresses, and you're the slave.' She took the belt from his jeans and used it to shackle his left hand. Then she stood back and looked at him.

Now she began to understand the sensation that excited Maxwell. She felt all powerful and omnipotent. Jason was helpless to do other than submit to her every whim. Before attempting to touch him, she slid out of her thong, and gave him the full benefit of her pubes, stroking the fair bush and inserting a finger into her crack. She withdrew it, wet with moisture, and ran it under his nose.

'Oh, God, Freya! Do what you like with me, but get on with it,' he begged, and she was gratified to see his penis engorged with desire, weeping tears from its single eye.

She slapped it, hard. 'What did I tell you to call me?'

'Ouch! Mistress!'

'That's better.' She leaned over and ran her tongue over his fiery glans.

He raised his hips, straining towards that exquisite touch, but Freya didn't intend to satisfy him. This was far too exciting. She took her mouth away. 'Bitch!' he muttered.

'Don't be rude, or dare question your mistress.' She smacked his thighs with all her force, while he strained against his bonds, swearing. She leapt from the bed, glaring down at him, 'All right. If that's your attitude, I may just leave you there tied up. You've got one hell of a boner and won't even be able to wank.'

'No, Freya, I mean mistress … don't go. I'll do anything you say.'

Slowing, as if considering the matter, she returned and knelt across his hips, a leg on either side, her sex open and on display. She could smell her own arousal and guessed that he could, too. Sitting back on his thighs, she opened her vaginal lips and her swollen clitoris poked out. Wetting her middle finger, she stroked it, rubbed and toyed with it, passion rising, her little organ ready to explode.

He was watching, and she used one hand to pinch her nipples, adding to the fire in her loins. To have him restrained made the feeling more intense. For the first time ever, she was in control, not the men she'd been with, so convinced of their superiority just because they had a dick. Well, so had she, or the equivalent, an organ many times more sensitive and capable of giving intense pleasure, if treated in the right way. Let him watch and learn.

'You like what you see?' she whispered. 'You want to poke me? I may let you, and just in case I do, I want your prick covered.' She took a condom from its packet and slipped it over his throbbing member. 'There. Now I'll get on. I'm right on the edge and you can watch me come.'

She threw back her head and concentrated on the ache within her that demanded satisfaction. This time she needed rough handling and rubbed her clit vigorously. The intense feeling took over, impossible to check and orgasm shook her from cortex to womb. Without waiting for the spasms to die away, she seized Jason's cock and, sitting astride, lowered herself on it, sinking down and feeling her muscles contracting around it.

He yelped and thrust, pulling against his bonds and

coming in a fierce rush. She flopped down, her head resting on him. 'Jesus God! That was great!' he panted.

She crawled to the bed-head and released him. Even this act thrilled her, and she felt strong and resolute. She kissed Jason fondly. She had learned an important lesson that night, and poured drinks and enjoyed them with him while they rested before experimenting with sexual games again.

Chapter 10

'Find me a virgin,' Maxwell said, with a final slap of his broad hand across Lola's bare buttocks.

'A what?' She gasped, wriggling with pleasure.

'Surely you know, or is it so long ago that you were in that state of grace?' He tumbled her from his lap on to the floor. 'A woman who hasn't been penetrated by a man. Someone who has never had a cock inside her.'

'I know, I know.' She picked herself up, scowling. 'There's no need to be so bloody patronising. Why do you want one? I thought you said they were hard work and hardly worth the effort.'

He lay back on the bed, musing on which was the more comfortable, this divan with all mod-cons in his establishment in London, or the four-poster at Daubeney Manor, hundreds of years old and undoubtedly the scene of many a vigorous coupling. It amused him to see that Lola was angry.

He linked his hands behind his head, his palms still tingling from the vigorous spanking he had just meted out. 'I'm planning a party at the manor, a sort of Hellfire Club do, when we'll all wear costume of the period.'

'And why the virgin?' She was calming down, sitting on the end of the bed and caressing his feet.

'Oh, just a little whim of mine. I've been reading an account of a similar event in those days and thought it might be fun to copy it.'

'When?'

'The work's going well there and we'll soon be celebrating a wedding, that of Jennie and Armitage, though they'll not be invited to the party. I shall dispatch them on honeymoon and ship some of the staff from here down to there.'

His mind was busy with plans and he was hardly aware of Lola's hand creeping up his inner thigh and playing with his cock. 'Will you be asking Miss Prim?' she said, acidly.

'I suppose you mean Freya?' He knew exactly how to rile her. 'She's on holiday in Florence with that dickhead, Andrew Chalmers. She'll be back by then and I'll invite her.'

'And him?' Lola breathed on his helm and he began to harden.

'I don't think it will be quite his scene.' He spoke calmly, master of self-control.

'Such a shame *she* isn't the virgin you're looking for. Wouldn't that be fun?' Lola's tone of voice amused him greatly. She made no attempt to hide her jealousy and resentment

'It would indeed. But even so, she is an innocent, unaware of some of the sexy games we play. It should be good sport.'

'And I can join in?'

'Of course, my dear. How could I possibly manage without you?' He said this in such a manner that she wasn't sure if he spoke seriously or not.

'I don't think you could. And that's the truth.'

'You're a useful slave-slut, sometimes.' Her rounded, sun-tanned rump was raised as she leaned over him. He slapped it, a calculated stroke that titillated without causing much pain. She squirmed and sucked his cock into her mouth. He felt its tip nudging against the back of her throat.

She moaned and pulled out to say, 'I hope I'm indispensable, master.'

He pushed her away roughly, snapping as he rose, 'Of course you're not! You stupid slag!'

She fell to her knees and clung to his bare legs. 'Oh, master. I know I'm not worthy! Beat me! Punish me!'

Both were entering into the charade, their lust exacerbated by him acting the cruel master and her in the role of his submissive slave. This is the position in which he longed to place Freya, angry because she had chosen to go away with Andrew, ignoring Maxwell whenever they met on site. He had business in London, and had been there when she actually drove to Gatwick, or rather Andrew had. She would only be gone a few days, but it was enough to seriously rile Maxwell. He used Lola as a scapegoat, unfairly and on purpose. The more he behaved like this, the more she seemed to like it.

A stay overnight in the County Hotel, breakfast and an early start. The car was left there and they were collected by coach, and in a couple of hours Freya and Andrew were on the 'plane. Everything had gone like clockwork, a most civilised way to travel, no pack-packs and student hostels for them. The tour operator's hostess was there to welcome them aboard, and another to greet them at Florence air-port. A 'bus awaited, too, one that was to stay with them throughout the visit and, with forty other passengers, they were whisked off to the hotel in a select quarter of the city.

Their room had two single beds, was air-conditioned and of the usual impersonal kind, clean and adequate, with a bathroom en suite. It reminded her of an upper class version of the motel room she had shared with Jason. But she was in Italy, and the very air seemed to be filled with music. Looking from the window over a side street, she could see men working on a conversion, and they were singing.

Andrew came up behind her, arms clasping her as he said, 'What is it, darling?'

'It's so lovely here, and listen to the workman.'

'Every one a Pavarotti. Get ready for dinner, and we'll have a look at the other guests.'

Before they left she had rushed round the shops and equipped herself with new sun-tops, skirts and shorts as well as a couple of cocktail dresses. She showered and smoothed lotion into her skin, aware of Andrew watching her most of the time, quite openly, in no way salacious. He had also washed, shaved and changed, wearing a casual cream linen suit and open-necked shirt. He was charming, handsome, well-heeled — everything she could desire, but — and it was a big but. She had been more turned on by the scruffy, jeans clad Jason.

In the dining-room they were ushered to a table by a smiling, extremely polite waiter. He had all the swarthy good looks of Giovanni, and paid considerable attention to her. His accent thrilled her, and the way he called her *signorina.* The food and surroundings were excellent, as to be expected in a five star venue. The other tour members were, on the whole, older than her and there seemed to be a number of people travelling alone. After the meal, they went into a side room where the music expert hired to accompany them to the operas, gave a short talk explaining the plot of the one they were to see the next night, *La Tosca.*

Andrew was easy with people, a good conversationalist and was soon chatting with him, comparing other productions of the work. Others joined in, but Freya was more reserved, although she knew this dramatic piece very well. Andrew, however, arranged to meet some of them in the bar for a last drink, and she went along, easing herself into the situation as a cat will in new surroundings.

The air was balmy, and they sat on a terrace furnished with small round tables and large parasols that would keep it cool by day. Smoking was permitted there and Freya lit up, glad to find that she wasn't alone; several others produce cigarettes. She had a feeling of unreality. Only a few hours ago she was in England, now her feet were on Italian soil. Tomorrow she would be seeing *La Tosca* on the shores of the lake near Puccini's villa. It seemed almost unbelievable. She should be able to forget Maxwell, but she found this impossible. He haunted her like a spectre and she couldn't help wondering what he would make of it all.

Back in their room, Andrew was on a high, chatting non-stop while they undressed and occupied one of the beds. He was already aroused, but Freya would have preferred to sleep, though felt obligated to show enthusiasm. The trip had cost him a bomb and he deserved that she was appreciative. She had another drink and tried to switch of her bothersome analytical mind. It worked and she was able to go through the motions convincingly; after all, hadn't women faked orgasm since time immemorial and their partners had been none the wiser?

She had decided to keep a journal, and added to it when they got back from the opera at 2.30 in the morning. "What a day! We looked around Florence before setting off in the coach after lunch. It took us some time to get to Torre del Largo and the scenery was spectacular, so many mountains in the distance. The opera started at 9.30 in the evening in a huge open-air stadium holding thousands.

It was so romantic, night closing in and the moon rising over the stage. A riveting performance, especially by the baritone singing the role of the sardonic villain, Baron Scarpia. This character is so much more exciting than the hero, Mario. He's cruel and dominating, and gets his kicks by forcing a woman, rather than have her fall in love with him. Could it be that even in my earlier days I responded to the dominating master, in the same way that I do Maxwell?"

She closed the diary quickly when Andrew came into the room.

'Wasn't it amazing?' he enthused, hugging her close. 'And the whole thing is so special because we're here together. Let me show you how much you mean to me.'

There was no answer to that. Swept along by Puccini's passionate music, she was able to respond to him.

By the end of the following night, she was even more bedazzled. *Turandot*, the composer's last opera, was stunning in every way, the story set in old Peking, with a heartless princess, a bedazzled suitor, and a happy ending. It was no way spoiled by the fact that Puccini died before completing the last Act and this was finished by a student of his, from the notes he had left. Completely worn out by so much emotion, Freya fell asleep as soon as her head hit the pillow.

Sunday, and nothing planned, so they wandered to the Ponte Vecchia that spanned the River Arno. It was lined with shops, mostly jewellers, with accommodation above, just as it had been for centuries. And it was there that Andrew waxed lyrical.

'Darling, what a romantic city in which to get married. Let me buy you an engagement ring, here and now. What d'you say?'

Her heart plummeted. This man was offering her a splendid life, with everything that she could possibly want, except perhaps, the most important ingredient of all, that she should be gut-wrenchingly in love with him. She wasn't, no matter how hard she tried. But how to let him down gently?

'We couldn't possible do it so quickly. It would take planning…a wedding, I mean.'

'I'm not suggesting we do it yet, only that I buy you a ring. The planning can start when we get home.' He looked crest-fallen and she felt contrite. There was no way she wanted to hurt him. 'It's too soon. Please, Andrew, I need more time. I like my career and don't want to be any one's wife at the moment.'

He gazed down into the fast-flowing Arno. 'I wouldn't stop you working. And I swear I wouldn't expect you to turn into a housewife. Will you give it serious thought?'

'Of course I will. And thank you for asking me.' She cuddled against his side and looked into his face. 'I'm so glad to know that you're my friend.'

'But that's all, isn't it? A friend?'

'Come on. We need to see the art galleries.'

He brightened. 'I've got tickets from the hotel, so we shan't have to queue.'

She took his arm and they retraced their steps. 'You're a marvel, Andrew, you really are. You think of everything.'

'I like things to go smoothly,' he answered, squeezing her hand.

She smiled up at him, while thinking, Maybe this is the trouble. He's just too meticulous. It kills the excitement.

The *Galleria Degli Uffici* was out of this world, and

she wandered through it in a daze. How extraordinary to actually see the original of Botticelli's *Birth of Venus*, painted so long ago, with others of the great masters. It was all too much to take in, and she realised that it was impossible in so short a time. They had one more day, and would be returning home. In a way, she would be relieved. Much as she had enjoyed the opera and the art and the extraordinarily beautiful city, it had been marred by Andrew's expectations and her own ability to fulfil them. The final night she occupied the spare twin bed, unable to bear his pain any more.

He was unusually quiet on the flight to England, and throughout the journey back to Blackheath. She felt awful, knowing that she had disappointed him. Then she recalled what she had been taught by her therapist—disappointment is of our own making. We have no right to expect anyone to fall in with what we have decided should happen. But this was small comfort when she glanced across at him as he drove in silence.

She was relieved when he pulled up outside her house and hefted her bag from the boot. She kissed his cheek in goodbye. 'I'll see you soon. It was lovely and thank you, but I'm really tired and need a good sleep in my own bed.'

'All right. I shall be back in the office tomorrow. I'll print out the photos on the computer and let you have copies.'

'Great! I'm longing to see the one you took of me standing near Puccini's statue in Lucca, outside the house where he was born. I shall visit the manor in the morning and will catch up with you later.'

It seemed strange to be talking like this when they had been so intimate for several days and nights. She was glad to turn the key in her own front-door and shut out the world.

'So…you haven't found it yet?' Maxwell was in the Great Hall with Grant.

'Found what?' Grant wanted to get on. There was still much to do. Sometimes Max could be annoyingly smug, especially if being secretive and evasive.

'Ah, ha! So you've not come across one of the manor's greatest mysteries?'

'Get to the point. The roofers are waiting instructions.'

Grant was feeling edgy. Freya had been acting strangely before she went away. Women! he thought. Difficult to understand. She'd been off with him ever since he found her in the pool. Not that he'd been pleased about it either. She had gone down in his estimation. He was puzzled by her lack of self-respect. And now there was Max, wasting time with silly questions.

'Think grotto,' Maxwell continued.

'You've shown me that. A place where the aristocratic nobs used to hold parties. Freya has seen it, too.'

'That's not all. There's more. I suggest you go down there and poke about a bit. When you find it, and I'm sure you will, tell no one, but come and see me.'

'Whatever. You're the boss, 'Grant answered, while thinking, we got on with the work much better when he was away in London.

He had to admit that Max had roused his curiosity and, after giving instructions to his team, he made his way to the folly. It was impossible not to recall how he had gone there with Freya. This was when they were getting on reasonably well. He regretted the lack of accord that had existed between them lately. As for her going away with

Andrew! Was there no end to the woman's philandering? Not that he gave a damn! But he changed his mind when in sight of the temple, deciding he would wait until she returned and go down with her, repeating what Maxwell had said.

Freya was due back at the end of this week and he tried to put her from his mind. There was still a lot to do, but he found her impinging on his thoughts and, cross and unsettled, he decided to go over to Bristol that night, look up Sally, one of his casual girl-friends and have a night of rampant sex. No commitment or sentimentality, just pure, unadulterated lust. That's all he needed to rid himself of the aggravating Miss Freya Mullin.

He rang Sally on his mobile and she seemed glad to hear from him. The drive to Bristol during the rush hour was tedious, but he garaged his car and met her in a pub near Park Street. He had forgotten that she was such good company, a lecturer at the university, with no baggage and a free and easy attitude towards relationships.

Back at his place, a house built from the profits from the slave-trade, they went to bed without preamble. He was hard as a rock, needing sex badly, and Sally appreciated his ardour. She was in her thirties and a good-looker, popular with the men but had not yet married, although having plenty of offers. Grant hoped she wasn't holding a torch for him, but she gave no indication of this, happy with straight-forward coupling or ready to enjoy giving him blow jobs and have him go down on her. It was hearty, healthy and uncomplicated and they parted early next morning to go about their respective activities, making no plans to meet up in the near future.

Grant drove to Blackheath wondering why all relationships couldn't be so simple, but he was aware of impatience to get back. Freya would be at Daubeney Manor.

Italy seemed a million years ago. Freya missed the warmth, but rejoiced in her own bed, familiar surrounds and, if she was honest, the opportunity to see Maxwell again. She went straight to the manor, putting off facing Andrew until the afternoon. The first person she saw was Jennie, all of a flutter with excitement about her impending wedding.

'Oh, Mr Sinclair has been ever so good. He's letting us have the reception here, and is providing caterers and has given us a generous bonus so that we can go away on honeymoon to Spain and stay in a posh hotel. You'll come and see us get spliced, won't you, miss?'

Her happiness was infectious and Freya envied it. Why couldn't her expectations be as simple? Was it because Jennie was older and prepared to accept what she could get? Or were her feelings for Jim Armstrong genuine? She rather thought they were.

'I'd love to. What about Danny?'

'He's going to be best man and will stay with his mates while we're away. He's off to university come October and Mr Sinclair has offered to finance him. He's so kind.'

This was an unexpected side of Maxwell's character and Freya wondered if she had misjudged him. Just because he had a bizarre taste in sexual activities didn't necessarily mean that he was a bad person, did it?

Stop it, she told herself firmly. Don't soften.

But he was the first person she bumped into as she emerged into the Hall. 'Freya.' He spoke her name without a flicker of emotion. It could have been one of the gardeners he was addressing.

172

'Yes, I'm back.' The banal statement covered a multitude of feelings, the chief of which was a heady desire to fling herself into his arms.

'And how was Florence?' He hadn't moved, yet she felt as if he was standing close beside her.

'Fabulous.'

'The opera?'

'Wonderful.'

'So you enjoyed the trip?'

'Oh, yes, thank, you.'

They could have been total strangers who had never shared intimate moments. Best to keep it that way, she thought, and made to continue walking. He moved swiftly and detained her with a hand on her arm. 'Have you seen Grant yet?'

'No. Why?' She went to shake him off but his grip tightened.

'I've set him a task. Daubeney has several interesting features not usually apparent. He's to search out one in particular, and I suggested that you should go with him.'

'Isn't this a colossal waste of our time? What is it? Some feature of historical significance?' She wished so much that he would let her go or that someone would interrupt them. Donna or Hilary were always hanging around him, but not when they were sorely needed, as now.

'I think so, and so will you…when you find it. If you have problems with this, I might take you there myself.'

'And Grant?'

He released her so suddenly that she stumbled. 'He's somewhere about. When you find him, tell him I've spoken to you.'

God, he's an arrogant pig! She fumed, but felt more

alive than she had for days, even when contemplating seducing the Giovanni-look-alike waiters in the hotel.

She went on a tour of inspection, taking note of what had been done during her absence. The builders were skilled and pains-taking, and the work was progressing satisfactorily. Eventually she came upon Grant. She saw the top of his hard-hat first. He was halfway down a manhole connecting with the drains. He heaved himself out and rubbed his hands down the sides of his dungarees.

'Hi there. The wanderer returns. Everything kosher?' His keen eyes seemed to strip away pretences, making her uncomfortable.

She decided to cut to the chase. 'I've seen Maxwell and he mentioned some mysterious part of the manor that we've not yet unearthed. It seems to afford him a great deal of amusement. Apparently he has already discussed it with you.'

The sun was shining down on them in this quiet spot, reminding her of Italy and its joys and frustrations. Grant stretched, squinting up at the sky. 'Nice day. I suppose you'll go skinny-dipping again with his nibs?'

'No. I have work to do.'

He grinned at her.' Does that including diving down into the grotto with me?'

'Not today. There are more important things needing my attention.' The ice in her voice could have sunk the *Titanic.*

'Goddamnit! If you aren't the most feisty, stubborn female I've ever met!' He was half laughing, part annoyed. 'What's wrong with me? Have I got the plague or something?'

'Not as far as I'm aware.' Freya made to move off, but he stood in front of her.

'Look here. We've got to work together for a while longer. Wouldn't it be better if we got on? How about a drink tonight? We can go to Charlie's pub, if you like.'

'I already have a date.' She hadn't, well not a definite one, but she guessed that Andrew would want to see her and she felt guilty about him. Anyway, she didn't want to spend the evening arguing with Grant. She'd done enough of that in the past, when they were at university.

'Then I double dare you to enter the mysterious grotto, and surprise Max by what we unearth.' He looked her straight in the eyes, and what she read there was a shock. She recognised a resurgence of the camaraderie they had once shared.

'Oh, all right. Anything to stop you going on about it,' she answered ungraciously and set off in the direction of the folly.

Chapter 11

The folly was as enchanting as Freya remembered. Fresh from Italy, she could see even more clearly how the one-time owner had been inspired to recreate a little piece of it here. She paused on arrival, remarking to Grant, 'Maxwell should allow it to be open to the public. It's almost his duty to do so and terribly selfish to keep it to himself.'

'Maybe you can persuade him. He seems to have taken a shine to you.' Grant was already shifting the slab over the entrance to the grotto.

'Don't be daft!' She could feel herself blushing. 'I hardly know the man.'

'You aren't the only one.' He gave a final heave, revealing the aperture. 'Come on, if you're coming. Though I don't know what he's blathering on about. I gave it a good look over before and found nothing unusual. Put your helmet on.'

She did so, saying, 'I went down there with him. It was weird.'

This was the understatement of the year. Weird wasn't the word to describe how Maxwell had blindfolded her and chained her wrists and brought her to pleasure's peak before taking her forcibly. There was no way she was going to tell Grant about this.

By the time she reached the tiled floor he was already flashing his torch, picking out colours and gilding and every rich and luxurious feature, lingering on the manacles fastened to one wall. He grunted. 'I saw these first time off. Looks like someone got their jollies in kinky ways. What d'you think?'

'I guess so.' There was nothing else to say, memories

176

surging back.

'Have you ever tried it? Being tied up and whipped?'

'It's not my thing.' She wandered around, using her own torch, careful not to disturb the furnishings, couches and carpets, though judging some of them to be recent.

'I reckon his nibs has all ready begun to use it. Bet he'll hold riotous parties down here. D'you thinks we'll get an invite?' Grant was exploring further, going deeper into the cavern-like structure.

'Maybe.' She followed him, disturbed by her surroundings and wanting to keep close to him. The place was redolent of Maxwell.

Grant lit a dozen candles, and the smell of melting wax permeated the air. 'I guess he'll have it wired for electricity soon,' he remarked, beginning to take an inventory.

Freya got out her note-book. 'Anything new?'

'Not yet.'

She watched him as he scrutinised everything, calling out his findings to her. The years rolled back and she remembered similar occasions when they were students and had been sent on surveys. So much had happened to her since then; her father's death, her grief when she had buried herself in her career, her first full on relationship which had been with Carl, and the subsequent let down. Her recent exploits with members of the opposite sex were out of character and she wasn't exactly proud of them, and there was still the problem of Andrew to be sorted.

She kept close to Grant. Although usually quite at home in spooky nooks and crannies, this place unnerved her, but wild horses wouldn't have made her confess this to him. Above all she must keep her cool. Her torchlight emphasised his wide shoulders and helmeted head. She caught the scent of him, his personal body odour and hair. It was pleasant, manly, and hadn't altered with time. It was a pity that they disagreed on daily matters because she knew they were alike in many ways, both filled with an avid interest in all things ancient. One might almost say dedicated to the pursuit of knowledge.

He stopped suddenly and she stumbled against him. He didn't move and neither did she. It seemed right to be touching. 'See this tapestry,' he said, and his voice was steady. 'I wondered about it before. It's large and fixed to the wall, and the subject is obscene, satyrs and nymphs cavorting in the woods. Look at the size of that guy's dick. That's a dong to be proud of. I wish mine was as big.'

He was speaking at random and she knew that he was as affected by the feel of her body as she was by his. It was stupid. Asking for trouble. Yet she couldn't help it and neither, she guessed, could he. 'Whoever painted it had a vivid imagination,' she managed to say.

He stood stock still and didn't turn to look at her, then, 'Freya, this is ridiculous. What are we doing, denying something strong that has been with us for years.'

'I don't know what you mean,' she lied.

He swung round and clasped her in his arms. 'You do. You can't deny this,' and he swooped and kissed her full on the lips.'

She twisted her face to one side, shouting, 'What the hell d'you think you're doing?'

'What I should have done long ago. Less talking and more fucking.' He kissed her again, deeply this time, forcing her mouth open under his, their tongues meeting.

178

Freya's womb ached and her clit tingled. She was aware that her panty gusset was damp. Had she taken leave of her senses? Was it Maxwell's influence in this place that was making her vulnerable?

Grant's free hand was at the waistband of her jeans, opening the zipper, diving inside while he muttered, 'Ah, this is what I've always wanted to do...to comb my fingers through your pubes.' She didn't attempt to stop him as he did just that.

It was a blissful sensation, in no way embarrassing or producing within her any sense of shame. Now he had her pressed against the tapestry, leaning on it to give himself purchase. Then he suddenly stopped caressing her. 'What's wrong?' she came down from the heights to ask.

He let her go and she hitched up her jeans. 'It's this tapestry. It's fastened to the wall, but I'm sure there's something behind it. Help me move it.'

Sex had been over-borne by archaeology, and Freya was caught up in it, too.

To their surprise the tapestry left the wall easily. 'It's been moved recently,' she said. 'There's no dust or cobwebs and look, there's a door behind it.'

He tried the handle. 'And it's locked, bolted on the inside I shouldn't wonder.'

'We can't break through, can we?'

'Not without his permission, but my guess is that he knows all about it and has already used it. I expect it leads to the house.'

'A tunnel under the ground?' Freya helped him replace the tapestry. 'What do we do now?'

'You present a report to him and we'll take it from there. Meanwhile, shall we go back to where we were interrupted?' He pulled her into his arms, but she pushed him away with her hands flat against his chest.

'I don't think so … not now …maybe not ever.' Her control was hard won but she stuck to it.

He let her go abruptly. 'OK. If that's how you want to play it, but I'm sure that the end will be the same. You and me are destined to get it together.'

Maxwell had rarely enjoyed himself so much. Guessing that Freya and Grant would go the grotto without delay, he had taken the secret way from his study and entered the shrine. From there it had been a matter of minutes to reach the door behind the tapestry, originally devised by Lord Sebastian. Maxwell had read his diary over and over, feeling that he actually knew the man, though this was an impossibility

He had used a dim torch and was as quiet as Sebastian's wraith itself, standing behind the door and listening to everything. What was said, even those intimate words that presented him with such a vivid picture of what was taking place between his surveyors. So, Grant *did* fancy her. Maxwell had suspected as much. As for Freya? She seemed utterly confused as to her desires, making her doubly intriguing.

Standing there in the dark, hardly daring to breathe, his cock swelled within his chinos. He wanted so much to watch them and promised himself that one day soon he would do exactly that. Themes for his proposed party ran through his brain as he stroked his phallus and strained his ears to hear their slightest breath or movements. He shrank back when Grant found the door. The fun was over, for the time being, and he retreated up the passage, well pleased with the afternoon's events.

Grant and Freya said no more as they left the folly, he to see to his workmen and she to make a report on her lap-top and e-mail it across to Maxwell. It was nearly six o'clock and she must face Andrew very soon. As she drove home she scolded herself. 'You're turning into a bloody nymphomaniac. No man is safe within a mile of you.'

Indoors, she made time to phone Moira and pour out her troubles, but all that lady did was applaud her actions. 'I'm glad to hear it,' she said. 'It's time you had a ball. Doesn't do any harm to try out the goods before settling on one. There's no hurry, pet. I've had dozens of blokes and now think I've found the one.'

'Giovanni?'

'Yep. We might even get hitched. Will you be a bridesmaid?'

'You're not serious?'

Moira gave a throaty chuckle at the other end of the line. 'I might be. You'll be the first to know.'

Andrew rang Freya as she came out of the shower later. Wrapped in a towel, she picked up the phone. 'Can I come round tonight?' He asked. 'I've printed out the photos. There are some good ones of you.'

'All right, but I don't feel like cooking,' she temporised.

'Not to worry. We can send out for a take-away.'

So cool a conversation, she thought as she dried herself and, naked, sat at the dressing-table and 'did her face'. This was always a time of reflection and she never hurried over it. The trouble was that she wasn't in love with any of them. Not in that crazy way that fills one with an exhilarating feeling of walking on air, romping among the clouds, deliriously happy because one was about to see the beloved object of this insanity. She had felt that about Carl, and look where it had got her.

Satisfied that her make-up was just so, she dressed casually in jeans and a lightweight sweater. It was warm enough to wear thronged sandals. She got out the mugs and instant coffee. No alcohol. She didn't want him to find an excuse for not driving home that night. This was going to be an awkward meeting. How could she explain her feelings without hurting him? This was impossible, but it had to be done. Although expecting it at any moment, she jumped when the door-bell rang.

'Hello, darling,' he said as he stepped over the threshold. 'It seems ages since I saw you.'

There was no answer to this, but she accepted his greeting kiss on the cheek and led him into the sitting-room. 'We need to talk,' she said bluntly, unable to put it any other way.

He sat down and held out an envelope. 'Take a look at these first. They came out really well.'

She didn't want to be reminded of the holiday, but took a cursory glance. It brought it all back, the sun, the music, Andrew's expectations. She laid the photos down and said, 'They're great. Would you like a cup of coffee?'

His face was serious as he grabbed her hand and said, 'What's wrong? Have I done something to upset you?'

'No! Oh, no. It's not you … it's me.'

'How so?'

'I can't explain. It's just that I'm not ready for a steady relationship yet. It's too close to Carl. I have to manage on my own for a while.' All the time she was thinking, what a lame excuse. That's not the true reason and you know it. How would you react if it were Maxwell there instead?

182

'Take as much time as you want.' Andrew was generous in the extreme. 'Just tell me that there's a glimmer of hope for me.'

'I think we'd better leave it for the time being. I'm not over Carl yet.'

He stood up. 'I'll go, if that's what you want. Keep the photos. I have another set.' His stoicism made her ashamed.

'I'm sorry, Andrew.'

'Don't be. Things will work out no doubt. We shall still have to work together.'

'And we'll still be friends?'

'Of course.'

She let him out into the night, closing the door after him and feeling dreadful. Not for her, but for *him*.

'Have you found her yet?' Maxwell stared across his desk at Lola, drumming his fingers on the surface.

'Who?' She stopped buffing her nails to look at him.

They were alone in his study, her flying visit necessitated by a television celebrity show in which they were both appearing. It was a late night and sophisticated, and they needed to get their heads together to discuss what they were going to say. Her agent was behind this, and so was his. Maxwell had a new book due out and she was about to shimmy down the catwalk wearing the new collection by a prestigious designer.

'The virgin,' he grated.

She pretended to have forgotten. 'Ah, yes, master. The virgin. Well, they're pretty rare these days. Must it be a fully fledged one? Won't a fake do?'

'No. Surely there's some empty-headed, ambitious

183

bimbo who has been hanging on to her cherry, waiting for the highest bidder?'

'I'll spread the word.'

'It will be worth her while, both in cash and as a career move. Do it, Lola. But now, come over here and give me a blow-job. I saw something today that made me horny as hell.' He swivelled his chair to one side so that she could kneel between his legs and perform fellatio.

Lola licked his tool from root to tip, then sucked it like the most delicious ice-cream, holding off, coming on, rousing him just the way he liked it. She looked up into his face and observed, 'You certainly have got a monumental hard-on. What was this something that excited you so much?'

'None of your business,' he snapped and pushed her head down to his groin. 'Just get on with it and then get out.'

'Am I not to stay the night?'

'Maybe. It depends on how much you please me.'

'You're a hard bastard,' she muttered, before tonguing his helm again.

'Shut up, slave.'

Freya did not sleep well and got up with a muzzy head. Strong tea proved an antidote and, once showered and dressed, she felt ready to face the day. Fortunately there was no need for her to see Andrew yet, the manor would keep her busy. Donna was waiting for her.

'Mr Sinclair received your e-mail and he wants to see you right away,' she announced loftily, barely bothering to hide her dislike.

Freya found it amusing. How dreadful it must be to harbour such strong feelings for a man who was simply her boss, although there seemed to be a little more behind it. Did Maxwell sometimes use her for sex when there was nothing else on offer? Freya wouldn't put it past him. Everything was a game to him, and every person his puppet. His arrogance was truly over-whelming.

'Where is he?' she asked, walking past her. She could see Hilary hovering about in the background.

'In his study.' Donna used that sniffy voice she reserved for Freya who wondered how she got on with Lola.

Irritated yet amused, she felt quite sorry for her. Donna was in the same position as a dog waiting for crumbs to drop from the master's table. Hilary, too, acted in this subservient manner. Did he hope for Maxwell's favours? Could there be a kind of ménage a trois existing between them? Freya felt that there was nothing left to shock or surprise her. Whatever the score, two pairs of eyes watched her like hawks as she tapped on the study door.

'Come in,' said Maxwell.

The sunlight was dazzling, pouring in at the large, diamond paned windows, set in bays with padded seats running round them. For a moment she was blinded to Maxwell who rose to greet her, a print-out in his hand.

'It arrived OK? I'm never quite sure if I trust modern technology,' she said, trying to turn it into a joke and deny the fact that her heart had lodged somewhere in her throat.

'Indeed yes, and it's very thorough. You found the door behind the tapestry.'

'You knew it was there?' Of course he did, the bugger! She thought angrily. He likes to get everyone at it. A control freak if ever I saw one!

'I discovered it when exploring. I've found a map of the foundations, left by Lord Sebastian Bartram, one of the former owners. And his journal as well, all most enlightening.'

'But you wanted Grant and me to find it, too. What was this? Some kind of test to prove our ability?' She felt like a mouse being tormented by a cat.

'Not at all. I thought you might enjoy the mystery.'

'So will you unlock the door and take us through?'

'I'd like you to come with me first.'

'When?'

'There's no time like the present. Don't pretend that you wouldn't like to put one over on him.'

Why wasn't I prepared for this? She thought. I might have known he'd have something up his sleeve. Now what do I do? He's right, of course, professional rivalry does exist between Grant and me. It's par for the course. 'Are you ready to put it on display for the public?'

'Have uncouth tourists roaming among works of art they won't understand? The idea repels me.'

'But you like to teach, don't you? Isn't this what your books and lectures and telly programmes are about?' She prayed that she hadn't been mistaken in admiring his incredible ability for making plain facts exciting.

'Of course I do. Why don't you come and take a look, then tell me what you think?' It was an offer that any historian worth her salt couldn't refuse.

'All right. Show me this amazing find,' she said.

He went to where one of the bookcases met the chimney breast. His fingers moved along the lavish ornamentation and a portion moved slightly. Freya watched as he opened it further, revealing a narrow aperture. 'A secret passage,' she said, interest honed. 'Where does it lead?'

'To the folly…eventually.'

'You mean there's more?'

'Take a look.'

He stood aside and she peered into the darkness beyond. He supplied her with a torch and went in first, holding out his hand to aid her. *De ja vu.* She thought cynically. Haven't we done this somewhere before? The steps ended in a passage.

'This leads to the folly, I assume.'

He had retained his hold on her hand. His fingers were warm and strong and well-shaped. 'It does. Excavated by Lord Sebastian, and whilst doing so, he discovered this.' He stopped at a door, opened it with a key from his pocket and led her in. The torch light moved over objects that flashed, grew more distinct as he lit candles, and rendered Freya speechless.

'A shrine?' She managed at last.

'I think so, and he writes about his discovery in his journal. Roman in origin, it seems. The manor must have been built on the site of a villa.'

'I agree with you, but it needs to be dated properly.' Freya was on her knees, examining the mosaic floor. 'It must have been buried for years.'

'It seems so, but when he restored it he made a careful inventory of its contents. It appears to be dedicated to Pan.'

'And there are other gods and goddess, too. It's amazing, and look at the offerings that were made centuries ago, jewels, gold cups. Has anyone else seen this?'

'Jeff Plover. He's an expert and agrees about its age.'

She had momentarily lost her suspicions of him, concentrating on this extraordinary find. 'You'll want me to make a report and hand it to Andrew?'

'I'm not sure. I rather like having it to myself.'

Back came the doubts. 'It's up to you, of course, but I'm sure the historians would be more than just interested, to say nothing of the public. It could be a very important discovery.'

'Sebastian concluded that it pleased Pan to have maidens' deflowered in his honour and their virginity dedicated to him.'

Freya detected underlying excitement in his voice. She was thankful that she no longer possessed her hymen 'You'd like to have been in his shoes?'

He touched Pan's upright phallus reverently. 'It might be wise to propitiate such a powerful deity. Sebastian thought so, and regularly promised marriage to innocent servant girls if they would consent to attend his orgies and give themselves to him. He had no intention of carrying out his promise, and the girls were dismissed as soon as he had done the deed and presented proof to Pan. It's all there in his diary.'

'What a bastard!' Freya fumed. 'Using his power and position for his own pleasure. I hope he rots in hell!'

'That's a bit harsh, isn't it? The girls must have been very simple to believe him, or very ambitious, seeking to climb beyond their station.'

'I don't care. I don't like him and suggest you hand your findings over to British Heritage right away.'

'Oh, dear, Miss Mullin, have I upset your sensibilities?' he mocked, his mouth set in a taunting line, his eyes narrowed as he watched her.

'Not at all.' She gathered herself together, though still fascinated by Pan and his enormous phallus.

All those centuries ago a worshipper had built this special place for him. Had the Roman who constructed the shrine also sacrificed virginity to please him? Is this what Maxwell intended to do, driven by the need to make obeisance, just in case there was anything in it, or simple carrying out his own cruel desires? Lord Sebastian must have been a man after his own heart.

'He never shared the secret with anyone else.' Maxwell continued, still staring at her. 'He entertained in the folly, screwed a virgin in front of his guests and then disappeared to propitiate Pan. After which he returned, sacked the unfortunate girl, and continued with the orgy.'

'Charming!' She retorted scathingly. 'And what happened to it when he died?'

'His heirs lost the estate through drinking and gambling and bad investments, but there were rumours and I met one of the last of his line who put me on track.'

'What about the labourers who helped him excavate? Didn't they talk?'

'He bought their silence.'

'And now?'

'It might be fun to restore the old sacrifice. *The Rites of Spring*, and all that.'

He's serious, she thought, a shiver running down her spine. 'Girls are more enlightened these days. I doubt you'd find one willing and able to go through this.'

'I'm working on it.' Suddenly he sobered, all laughter gone. 'I know you're anything but a virgin, but why don't we fuck…right here…in front of him?'

'No, thank you, Maxwell. It's cold and I'm not in the mood,' she lied, the novel idea taking root and sending fire coursing along her veins. He was just too attractive, despite his strange quirks.

'Don't give me that,' he mocked, and placed the torch on a ledge. Its beam threw Pan's dark silhouette against the wall. 'Come here, Freya. You know you want to.'

189

She decided to be frank. 'I find you intriguing and attractive, but know it would only lead to disaster for me. I'd prefer we kept it on a business leave.'

'Really?' He stepped closer and cupped her breasts in his hands.

Her nipples responded instantly, hardening as pleasure shot through them to her groin. 'Don't...please,' she gasped. 'This is insanity.'

'But fun, too,' he murmured, and his mouth came closer, lips engulfing hers, tongue forcing entry. This was her undoing. Why not?

There were plenty of reasons to refuse. He was untrustworthy, a player, into domination. But she was learning not to take sex too seriously. Just because she screwed a guy didn't mean that they were together for life. 'I can't. I don't want to.' She blurted out, pulling away from him.

'You will. And you'll enjoy it.' And before she could stop him he had tied her hands behind her. She felt the cold kiss of metal on her wrists. 'Now then, let's have no more of this girlish reticence.'

Her skirt was whipped up and her panties off, and he was between her thighs, nuzzling her clitoris. She could have kicked out, struggled, protested, but the pleasure was too acute. He opened her wide, his fingers in her vagina, his tongue playing with her nubbin. Nothing was of importance but that he continue until she climaxed. He has taken command, tormenting her by merely breathing on her throbbing organ, then sucking it fast and steady and holding off again until she begged.

'Go on! Don't stop! Oh! Ah!'

She was shuddering, poised on the brink, while he chuckled, and licked her vaginal wings, ignoring her pleasure bud. 'You want it badly? You'd do anything for it, eh? Shall I bring you off, or shall I leave you? 'As he whispered, hovering over her cleft, his breath almost tipped her into ecstasy, but not quite. So near and yet so far.

'Please,' she sobbed.

'Will you be an obedient slave, carrying out my every command?' His tongue tip was poised over her clitoris, not quite touching it. She raised her pelvis but he refused to allow her swollen crest to contact his mouth.

'I'll do anything…anything…'

He closed over her, fingers stretching the labia apart, the clitoris standing proud like a miniature cock. His tongue worked swiftly over the crest and Freya went with the pleasure that rose through her loins, up her spine and into her cortex, flooding her with amazing sensations. She came to orgasm in a whirl of rainbow colours and throbbing feeling that was like nothing on earth or in heaven.

Her inner muscles contracted around him as he pushed his penis into her, up and up until it seemed he would penetrate her very heart. Her tethered hands were pressed against the wall behind her, legs hooked round his waist as he rode her to his own completion. She felt the surge of his spunk as it shot into the condom, and this echoed the rush of emotion that gripped her so that she wanted to cry and beg him to stay with her in this dark and holy place for ever.

CHAPTER 12

'OK. He's shown you this important find. So what! He took me down there, too, and yes, it is extraordinary.' Grant was speaking to Freya without looking at her. It was the first time she had bumped into him since that episode with Maxwell.

It occurred to her that maybe the two men had got it together, both into any kind of sex. She could believe it of Max, but not Grant. She couldn't see him being restrained and arse-fucked, though she had come to realise that anything was possible. One could never know what went on in someone else's psyche.

His eyes met hers and she read a question there. Was he thinking the same thing about her? She shifted her gaze, appearing to be absorbed in her list of things to do. 'Are you making out a report on the shrine?'

'When he gives me the go-ahead.' He suddenly switched from measuring the wall of the main bedroom, swinging round to her and saying, 'Why don't we get out of Blackheath for a few hours? Come to Bristol. We'll revisit the watering-holes of our student day and you can stay at my place, just across the road from the uni. No strings. Just the spare room. What d'you say?'

He had caught her at an all-time low. She needed a distraction, something to remind her of a time when she had high ambitions and a belief in the goodness of human beings. To be young and hopeful again, not scarred by cynicism.

'All right,' she said, without giving herself time to regret it.

'Shall I pick you up after work?'

'I'll drive my own car, then I can leave any time I want.' The expedition was likely to be fraught and she wanted an escape route.

It gave her something else to think about as she finished work and drove home. There, her mind filled with images of comparatively stress-free, youthful days, she packed an overnight bag and secured the house. All of Clive's possessions were gone and she had heard that he was living with someone else. Poor cow, she mused. Oh, he'll be great for a while, until the real bastard shows through the cracks.

As the French song went; *No. No regrets. No. I have no regrets.* And she meant it.

Grant was on time. He always could be relied to turn up when he said he would. She locked the front door behind her. 'All set?' he called put through the driver's window. 'Right. Then let's hit the road.'

They had timed it to avoid home going traffic. Freya had not been there for a while, preferring Bath if she wanted to do a spot of shopping. The Centre was busy and they drove up Park Street, the stately university building looming on their right, bringing back a wealth of memories. She followed Grant and arrived in an eighteenth century square surrounding a railed-in green.

Pulling in behind him, she switched off, saying, as she got out and secured her car, 'You've done well for yourself. We used to look at places like this and wonder if we'd ever be able to afford one. They were mostly flats then.'

'I bought Number 8 just before the prices rocketed. It was empty and I transformed it into what it would have been like originally, when some prosperous merchant had it built as his town residence. This was a select area in those days, not too far from the docks and the in coming slave-ships.'

'I don't like to think about that.' She followed him through the glass panelled door into the hall. The dado was of dark wood and the wallpaper a large-pattered William Morris design. The house breathed out a warm, friendly atmosphere.

He led her into a kitchen at the back, explaining, 'This used to be in the basement, but I found it too dark, so that's a laundry room now.'

It was modern, but in keeping with the rest, and had a door leading out to some steps which gave access to a small yard. It was enclosed by houses similar to this one. Little likelihood of sunbathing there. Grant switched on the kettle. 'Fancy a brew before we hit the pubs?'

Freya set down her bag. This was more pleasant than she had anticipated. 'That would be nice. Do you live here alone?'

He got out the tea-bags. 'No. I share it with a studious minded lecturer…Bob Evans. He works over the road.' He jerked his thumb in the direction of the university. 'And looks after this place when I'm away.'

'Where is he tonight?'

'Staying with his girl-friend. He'll be leaving me when they get married. That has a nice ring to it, hasn't it? Getting married, settling down and having children.'

'You can't be serious. Not a free agent like you.'

'You'd be surprised.' He poured boiling water on the bags in two mugs, added milk and sugar, handed one over and pushed the biscuit tin towards her. 'Take a pew and then we'll have a guided tour of the homestead.'

Though confused by his former statement, she felt more comfortable than she had anticipated. The house wasn't overly tidy, just normal and, as they went from room to room, she found it decorated with taste and flair. It was larger than it appeared from outside, consisting of two levels above the ground floor and a substantial attic that would have once been the servants quarters. He pushed open the door of a room overlooking the green.

'I've put you in here.' It had a Regency theme, much in keeping, with a wide, comfortable looking bed. 'There's an en suite bathroom. I'm next door.'

They went there and this proved to be a surprise and she admired the Egyptian ambience, drapes, couch, pictures and ornaments smacking of the time of the pharaohs. 'This is lovely,' she exclaimed. 'One of my favourite periods. It reminds me of a set for Verdi's opera *Aida*.'

'Does it? I wouldn't know. I'm not an opera buff, but, yes, I'm smitten with the tombs and all things from that time. Want to try my bed? It may look sparse but I can assure you the mattress is as modern as tomorrow.'

There was an amused glint in his eyes, and something else, too. Her hackles went up warningly. It was rather too intimate a situation and she changed to subject abruptly. 'What about that drink?'

'*What* about it? Dear me, I'd almost forgotten, enthralled to have you in my clutches.'

Was he teasing? She couldn't be sure and pushed past him, heading for the stairs. It was all just a little too cosy and she could feel herself slipping into it.

They walked down to the quay, a popular venue with cafés and public houses, encouraging sight-seers who wanted to admire the old ships moored there. It hadn't changed a lot since Freya was a green girl coping with the stresses and strains of living away from home and sharing a house with several other students.

The evening was fine and dry and it was a case of 'do you remember?' as they found a favourite pub, and ordered two pints of scrumpie, that bland tasting, extremely alcoholic Somerset cider. It had gone up in price tremendously. They agreed that they could never have afforded it in the old days. It was cheap then, one of the only drinks they could buy from their meagre allowances.

The Griffin hadn't altered much, apart from NO SMOKING signs inside. They occupied one of the round, marble-topped tables facing the river. It ran steadily downstream, heading for Avon-mouth and the sea. Grant leaned over and flicked his lighter. Freya inhaled the smoke from her cigarette. She had fallen right back into how it had once been when they were mates. Maxwell would have been out of place there. In fact no one fitted in as perfectly as Grant. The cider slipped down, deceptively smooth, and the idea took root.

One or two acquaintances greeted him, and he nodded in response, but there was none of the old gang. 'What happened to them all?' she asked, watching the play of street lights on the river and realising how much at home she felt.

'Who knows? I've bumped into a few at odd times. Some are married, some divorced, others working abroad or in other parts of the country. We've not kept in touch. Water under the bridge, I guess.'

A jazz band was playing in the lounge bar, and the music drifted through the open door. Though not really her bag it, too, was reminiscent of other, talented local groups she had heard in the past. 'They're good,' she remarked, shaking her head in refusal of another drink.

He nodded, silent of a sudden, as if the cider was getting to him. It had the affect of making the drinker ebullient or melancholy. Freya had had enough, suddenly tired and needing to sleep. 'Shall I ring for a cab?'

'It's up to you.' He really had gone into a mood and she was glad when the taxi arrived and whisked them up Park Street and turned left into the square where he lived.

He paid the cabby and, once they were in the hall, suddenly swept her into his arms, saying, 'Let's not waste any more time. I want you and you want me.'

She wasn't prepared for this, and certainly not for her response. He was so tall and muscular, his hair falling forward as he swooped down to kiss her, capturing her mouth before she had time to protest. That kiss destroyed her resistance, just as it had done in the grotto. She felt puny and insignificant, her breasts crushed against his muscular chest, her nostrils filled with the smell of him mingled with the scent of his blue Levi jacket. It was an irresistible combination. Her lips parted of their own volition, accepting his probing tongue. He tasted of Somerset's finest vintage.

I'm mad, she thought. He's not the one for me. Or is he?

He leaned his back against the wall, pulling her with him, and continued to kiss her, long and deep. Her hands were against his chest. She could feel the steady thud, thud of his heart, and was all too aware of the thickening behind his jeans. This had all happened before, and they taken it even further, would probably have gone for consummation, had the door not become evident behind the tapestry. So why stop now?

He moved, taking her with him, half-carrying her up

the stairs to his pyramid inspired room. He kicked the door shut behind him and laid her down in the bed. All tenderness and control vanished and he almost tore at her clothing. She helped him, caught up in the fever of desire. Off came her jacket, tee-shirt and jeans, leaving her in her bra and panties. Grant paused, feasting his eyes on her body.

'God, you're a stunner,' he muttered, sitting back on his haunches, not touching her. 'And you've been wasting all this on that prat Maxwell. Not only him. There have been others, haven't there? But none of them matter. You're here with me now.'

At this point she could have stopped him, but this was the last thing on her mind. She simply lay there, wondering what he was going to do next. 'It's odd to be with you like this after all these years,' she murmured, and it was a relief to be able to tell him anything she liked.

'It feels right and natural, but don't think for a moment that I'm a push-over. I guess that Max introduced you to domination. I can do that, in fact I want to try it right now.' He moved to the nightstand, opened a drawer and took something from it. He held out the leather covered object. 'Has be tried this on you? It's a paddle. I'll show you how it works.' He yanked off her brassiere and briefs, then rolled her over, ignoring her resistance.

She heard a swish, followed by pain that radiated across her buttocks. 'Ouch! Stop it!' she cried.

'Shut up!' He commanded, the all powerful male bending her to his will, and the paddle landed again, higher this time, making her shoulders burn.

He hit her twice more, and she started to glow, the feeling spreading to her loins. She was his to do with as he wished and she loved that feeling of submission, just as she had done with Maxwell. All decisions had been taken from her, freeing her from responsibility. Helpless in his strong hands, she rejoiced in being controlled.

When he stopped and forced her onto her back, she was aware of pain and desire mixed in a heady potion. She could trust him implicitly and lay, limp as a rag-doll, as he spread her thighs and gazed at her cleft, then touched the labial wings and swollen clitoris. She was wet and he spread the fluid over that sensitive organ. Freya moaned with need.

She looked up into his face, and was excited by the absorbed look in his eyes. He was concentrating entirely in giving her pleasure. He had unzipped and his cock protruded, a large, fully erect weapon ready to impale her and bring about his own release. With his free hand he pinched her nipples until she was almost screaming and he rubbed her harder, her clit throbbing, the pleasure intensifying until she suddenly exploded into climax. And it was then that he plundered her, his cock filing her to capacity, the helm butting against her cervix.

She needed this after such a powerful orgasm, and hugged him to her, taking all he could give, feeling him shoot his spunk into the condom. He rested across her, his weight pinning her to the mattress and she was content to have it so, her man trapping her beneath his powerful body, his drained sexual organ softening within her.

He kissed her neck and played with her hair, then pulled out and undressed, gathering her to him again and lying by her side. Words seemed superfluous. His arms enfolded her and she cuddled against his chest, no longer aware of the whys and wherefores, content to fall into a deep, peaceful sleep.

When they awoke it was a working day, and they breakfasted in silence and went their separate ways. Freya was lost for words and, so it seemed, was Grant. All the way back to Blackheath, she was going over last night's events. Would it lead to a relationship? Did she want it to? On the surface it would have everything going for it. They had similar backgrounds, interests and expectations. He was a far better bet than either Andrew or Maxwell and, she had to confess it, the magic was there, that chemical response without which no affair can flourish.

The manor was bustling. Jennie's wedding was next day. Freya She didn't see Grant, and Andrew was otherwise engaged, or so he said. She went about her duties quietly, wondering if Grant was avoiding her. Perhaps he hadn't intended to lose control and was regretting it. She was thankful that Moira was due to arrive that afternoon… Once she had taken pride in her home, decorating and titivating, holding dinner parties, but she had lost interest since Carl decamped. The truth was that she couldn't be bothered and this was worrying. She hoped that Moira would cheer her up.

'Have you got you're outfit for the wedding?' Was one of her first questions on arrival, Giovanni had been given the job of taking the cases to the guest room.

Freya was serving her coffee, her first demand, the second being a cigarette. 'I've something suitable. I'm glad Jennie included you in the invitations.'

'That was kind. I don't know her well, but the more the merrier.'

'She is so happy that I think she'd like the world and his wife to be there.'

'I can share her feelings.' Moira was looking decidedly

smug. She held out her left hand. A diamond flashed on her ring finger.

'You haven't done it? Not got engaged?'

'I have and it's to Giovanni. I shall soon be a respectable married woman. Will you be my bridesmaid?'

Freya was astonished. How could she ask her that when the three of them had shared a bed? It didn't seem right somehow. 'Well, I'll think about it. Congratulations anyway.' She set the coffee mug in front of her friend while wondering if she was the only person alive who had standards and wanted to preserve them.

'You sound a bit lukewarm.' Moira eyed her searchingly. 'What's up? Something have happened since I saw you last.'

Oh, hell, I suppose I'd better fill her in, Freya thought, then poured out the whole story concerning Grant.

'Good grief, you don't half get yourself into some tricky ones,' Moira exclaimed. Giovanni came into the kitchen just then. He bent over to kiss her. She touched the side of his face. 'Don't let him stop you,' she said to Freya. 'I don't keep any secrets from him now … well, not many. He has a good suss on relationships and will probably come out with something sensible. '

Freya went through it again, while Giovanni sat by Moira, twining his fingers with her. When Freya ran out of steam, he looked at her with his velvety brown eyes and said, 'Which of these men do you love?'

This floored her. 'I don't know. Maybe neither of them.'

'Then why are you so bothered? The right man will come along for you one day. I never thought I should be so lucky, but I've found Moira.' He reached up and tweaked her nipples and Moira giggled like a teenager…

She's besotted, Freya thought, shocked. I never thought

I'd see the day. It was apparent that she really had no time for Freya's problems. A woman in love, she was blind to everything except the object of her affection. Freya felt superfluous in her own house.

'I think I'll take this boy up for a siesta. Not that he needs his beauty sleep…he's beautiful enough as it is,' Moira said archly. 'Would you like to join us?'

This amazed Freya. How could she, when they were engaged and all? She excused herself. 'No thanks. Things to do. People to see,'

They disappeared and Freya fidgeted. She missed her friend's down-to-earth advice, but now it seemed she was otherwise engaged. Hearing their voices from above, and the sounds as they made passionate love, she took herself out into the garden. It wasn't true that she was busy, everything was arranged for tomorrow, and she allowed herself to dwell on Maxwell being at the register office. He had offered to be a witness. Then there was to be a shindig at the manor, where a reception was being held. She had heard rumours of a party he intended to throw that night, when the happy couple had departed. Then Donna had handed her an invitation, but was unforthcoming. Freya could only hazard a guess as to the nature of the celebrations.

She jumped when the phone rang, and then lifted it to her ear. 'Hello. This Freya Mullin.'

'Have you got your costume?' Maxwell's voice was unmistakable.

'What costume?' She was astonished to hear him.

'For the party in the grotto. It's an eighteenth century theme and everyone should be dressed accordingly. Come to the manor this evening and see what've we've got. Lola has hired outfits.'

'Oh, right. Thank you. What about my friend Moira and her bloke? They've come for the wedding.'

'Bring them along, too. See you then,' and he hung up.

I should have refused, she scolded herself when she had recovered. Why do I always do what he orders? She prayed that Grant might be there, needing him like a lifeline. You could ring him and find out, suggested her sensible self. I'm not grovelling to *him*, retorted the stubborn one.

Moira and Giovanni were up for it, rising early evening to shower, change and refuel their bodies with food. 'What's he up to?' She wanted to know when Freya told them about the costumes.

'It's for a party that's going on for his special guests after the reception.'

'In the house?' Moira ran her fingers through her tousled hair, the epitome of a woman who has just been thoroughly shagged by the man she adores.

'I presume it's in the folly and the grotto underneath.' It must no longer be a secret if he was taking his guests there, but she didn't mention the shrine.

'And we're to go there to try on costumes?'

'We'll do this at the manor. Lola has arranged everything, or so it seems.'

Moira gave her a sharp glance. 'Not jealous, are you?'

'Don't insult my intelligence.' Freya was prickly and wished they weren't going.

CHAPTER 13

'Darling, you look gorgeous!' Lola gushed when Maxwell had finished changing into costume.

He preened before the mirror, every inch the late eighteenth century beau. He would have graced the court of the Prince Regent. His buckskin breeches were exceedingly tight, emphasizing his manhood and ending below the knee where they joined black boots of the finest leather. His gold brocade waistcoat was short with wide lapels, his green velvet cut-away jacket had tails, and his high collar and cravat were pristine white. His hair was brushed into the fashionable Brutus cut of the day, falling forward over his forehead.

He could almost have been Lord Sebastian in person.

He felt like him, too, wondering if there was anything in the theory of reincarnation, but one thing annoyed him. They hadn't been able to track down a virgin.

He had to blame someone for this, and had been offhand with Lola, although she had done everything else possible to make this party a success. She came up to him, wearing a diaphanous, high-waisted dress, with tiny puff sleeves and a neckline that was so low it almost displayed her nipples. It was white, and she could have looked virginal, were it not for her wanton attitude.

She rubbed against him, pressing her pubis to his bulge. His hands came up, gripping her shoulders and pushing her away. 'I don't want this costume crumpled before the event. '

'All right, all right! Don't blow a fuse.' She rounded on Donna and Hilary who were attired as servants. 'And you'd better take those things off and keep them for tomorrow.'

Donna pulled a face behind Lola's back. She wore a sober dress with a coif and apron and he was attired in black, every inch the butler. They had been allocated the job of seeing that everything ran smoothly on the domestic scene once Jennie and Armitage had departed. 'We've got to go anyway,' she said. 'Loads to do.'

Freya arrived in the middle of this, having been shown to the apartment that was being used as a temporary dressing-room. Moira was taking note of everything, her journalist's nose twitching, while Giovanni accompanied her, amused by the antics of the English.

'Come in and join the fun, and your friends are welcome, too.' Max exclaimed, giving Freya the full benefit of his magnificence.

Her heart jumped and her hormones went on the rampage, but she was determined not to give way to them. 'So many costumes.' She nodded to where they occupied hangers or were spread across the bed.

'These are for us to choose from. My guests will supply their own.' He made an expansive gesture. 'Help yourselves.'

'Did you use some from the trunks in the attic?' she asked, vividly recalling their first time alone.

'I looked at them, but the period was too late. Nothing earlier than Victoria's reign.'

'I hired them from a London theatrical costumier,' Lola supplied, and seized Freya's arm. 'Let's find something suitable for you, and Giovanni darling, you'll look hot in an open-necked shirt with baggy sleeves, and tightest of tight breeches.' She was ignoring Moira, and Freya smiled, remembering the antipathy between them.

Freya was attracted to an ivory silk dress in true

Napoleonic style, reminiscent of the Empress Josephine. She held it against her. 'Can I try this on?'

'Of course.' Lola had already stripped off, nude now, her body glowing. Freya could not help admiring it, remembering the feel of Moira in her arms and wondering how it would be with Lola.

She searched for somewhere to change. There appeared to be no privacy, the others happily engaged in trying on this and that outfit, totally uninhibited. She chided herself for her shyness, very aware that Maxwell was watching her. She found a corner by the bed, kept her back turned and succeeded in slipping out of her clothes and into the dress, retaining her underwear. Then she realised that her bra showed and was forced to abandon it.

'That's perfect,' he said, coming across to her. 'You must pin your hair up, with little fronds over each ear, and add a stole. Flat heels are essential, sandal style. Did you now that fashionable ladies of that era dampened their petticoats so that they would cling to the legs and outline them?'

'I didn't. I wonder how many of them got pneumonia? Silly girls. risking their lives to please men,' she retorted pithily.

'That sounds like feminist speak.' He was teasing her, and her resistance wavered.

He left her, taking off his jacket and waistcoat and placing them carefully on a hanger. Now he was attired, like Giovanni, in a shirt with blowing sleeves ending in lace cuffs, his breeches fitting his lean hips neatly. It was a sight to addle a nun's brain. Lola was already romping on the bed with Jeff Plover who had also come along to be kitted out. She was showing off for the benefit of anyone who wanted to watch. They had moved the fancy-dress costumes and had the whole space to themselves, though not for long.

'Come on, Moira, bring that lovely man of yours over here,' she demanded, but Moira was reluctant to share him with anyone, particularly her.

'No thanks. We're happy on the sofa.' She embraced him possessively and they began to make love.

Maxwell looked at Freya and said, 'What about you? Fancy a little group sex?'

'No.'

'Are you sure?' He touched her breast and her skin tingled through the silk. Damn him, she thought, why does he make it so bloody difficult to say no?

'Yes, I'm sure.'

'Well, how about just the two of us?' He opened a door and she found herself in a walk-in wardrobe. It was dimly lit and contained racks for clothing and shelves for storage.

'I don't want to do this,' she protested, but while her head said no, her body insisted she carry it through.

Maxwell ignored her, enfolding her in his arms, lowering his head to kiss her, his probing tongue removing her last remaining scruples. He held her wrists behind her back, refusing to let her go, and his hard fingers were painful. Her senses responded to this, stirred by memories of other occasions when he had hurt and satisfied her. He was a wizard who knew how to please her every which way. The hard line of his penis pressed against his tight breeches and her flimsy dress. He leaned in further, bending her backwards, looming over her until she felt like putty in his hands.

He spoke against her cheek. 'You've been disobedient. I hear reports of you screwing other men.'

Her wrists were numb within his grip, her struggles futile. 'You don't own me.'

'Are you sure about that?' He released her momentarily, and then used a belt to secure her hands again. This, in turn, was attached to one of the shelves.

Next he pulled down her bodice and bared her breasts, nibbling at the nipples greedily. The feeling was too pleasurable to resist. 'Maxwell, why are you doing this?' She gasped. 'You have plenty of other women. I'm here to do a job, that's all. My private life is no concern of yours.'

'I find you entertaining, Miss Mullin. You try to be so prim and proper but there's a naughty girl beneath this pose. I'm simple helping you to release her.' He raised one hand and slapped her hard across the thighs.

She jerked, moaned, and was hopelessly aroused. Nothing would satisfy her but being impaled on his cock. He went on punishing her, his palm raining blows on her legs, arms and breasts, until the tears flowed and she was begging him to stop. 'Don't! Maxwell, please! No more!'

'Ask me to fuck you.'

'I can't do that. I don't want it …'

He chuckled and pinched her breasts painfully. 'Liar! Say it…'

There was nothing more she could do, nothing she wanted more than for him to take her as brutally as possible. 'All right. Maxwell, I want you to fuck me.'

'Say, please, master' he insisted.

'Please, master, will you fuck me?'

He did not untie her wrists, but lifted her skirt and exposed his engorged cock. Then he slid a hand between her legs and spread her moisture over her labia and clitoris, while she moaned and babbled, unsure of what she was saying; only knowing that she had to have a climax. He used his skill to bring her closer and closer to the point of no return until wave after wave of feeling mounted higher and higher and her orgasm broke in a multitude of sensations. Then he lifted her and drove his cock into her forcefully, chasing his own release.

Her vaginal muscles contracted round his girth and she could feel him pumping against her cervix. Something told her that never again in her whole life would she experience such a completely satisfying sexual experience.

He withdrew, removed the rubber that she had not been aware of, and tucked his penis back into his breeches. It was as if nothing untoward had taken place. He undid the belt, releasing her aching arms and sore wrists. She rubbed them, unsure of what to say. He smiled slightly and opened the door, standing back so that she might go first. The lovers were resting after their activities and Lola was asleep.

'Are you ready to go?' Moira asked, giving Freya a knowing glance.

'I'll get into my own clothes and then we'll be off,' she replied. 'I can't wait to get out of here.'

Freya had been unable to avoid coming into contact with Andrew during the week. Her conscience bothered her regarding him and, although he never reproached her, she felt awkward in his presence.

She was relieved when he said to her, quite casually as they were going over some papers in the office, 'I bumped into an old friend the other day. I used to work with her husband, but he died of cancer not long ago and she is bereft. I'd like to cheer her up, if that's possible, and am taking her to a concert at Bath Abbey.'

'When one door closes another opens,' she quoted, pleased with this turn of events.

'So they say.' He looked so much happier that she could do nothing but wish him well in her heart, and hope that the widow proved to be the woman he was seeking.

The next time Freya saw Maxwell was at the register office. Jennie looked radiant, wearing a cream jacket and skirt while her groom was elegant in a dark suit. So was Danny, hardly recognisable in his role as best-man. Freya found it hard to equate this grownup person with the denim clad lad she knew. It went without a hitch, and the bridal party returned to the manor where the Great Hall had been prepared for the reception.

Freya could not help admiring Maxwell for the way in which he had organised and paid for the couple's great day. He was an enigma, generosity itself when it suited him, but having this dark, secret side to his personality.

Jennie and James were popular and had many friends. The Hall rang with laughter, talk and congratulations and Freya envied them. She knew that deep within her was the desire to be a bride, though she would never have confessed it. She was a modern woman, wasn't she? Quite independent.

She searched the crowd for Grant, but he was nowhere to be seen. He had been avoiding her since the episode in Bristol, and she didn't know whether to be glad or sorry. Moira was there, flamboyant in chunky jewellery, hipster trousers and a tank top, and Giovanna was his usual handsome self. Freya felt lonely. She had no man to escort her and Maxwell was totally absorbed in playing the genial host.

It was all very traditional, the champagne, the speeches, the wedding-cake, although this was not a first for either of the bridal pair. When they left for the airport and their honeymoon, Freya was feeling tired and a little tipsy. Sparing no expense, Maxwell had supplied first-class vintages.

As soon as the last of the wedding guests had departed, he said, 'Right now, all those who are carrying on the entertainment get into their costumes for Act Three. My own friends will be arriving soon and the real party will start.'

Moira linked her arm with Freya's, saying, 'Come on, baby. In for a penny; in for a pound.'

'You say such strange things,' Giovanni complained. 'What is this "penny for a pound"?'

'Don't worry your pretty little head about it,' Moira soothed, kissing him.

There was an atmosphere of excitement and anticipation in the dressing-room. Freya found the ivory silk gown and put it on, remembering what Maxwell had said about her hair and shoes, although she didn't dampen her petticoat, thinking, Blow that for a game of soldiers! She wasn't quite sure what this meant, but it sounded good. The gown was revealing enough as it was and she added a cashmere shawl. This made her feel less exposed.

All was noise below as Maxwell's cronies started to arrive. There was food and drink left over from the reception and those who wanted were invited to tuck in. Freya crept down the wide staircase, staring at the motley crew who were attired in a variety of outfits. Many of them had conformed to Maxwell's idea of a Regency theme, but others had dressed to please themselves. There were several monks, a pirate or two, a ring-master with a troupe of girls pretending to be ponies, wearing harness and flowing manes and with tails stuck up their arses. Freya was astonished by the variety of fetish wear. Manacles and whips were in evidence and several lovely transvestites, as well as others who were obviously female, dressed in leather dominatrix gear. It was a world quite new to her.

Maxwell rounded everyone up, standing on the stairs and announcing, 'Welcome all. I'm now going to take you to the folly and introduce you to the delights of Lord Sebastian's grotto. Follow me.'

It was growing dusk and the evening was balmy. Freya thought Daubeney Manor had never appeared more beautiful, a gracious building that held secrets, nonetheless, and she was already privy to some of them. The chattering crowd trailed across the lawn to the copse, expressing excitement when they reached the temple. Maxwell had removed the slab and the entrance to the grotto was lit by flares in ornamental holders. It looked magical, and Freya wished it was to be used for some other purpose than an orgy, for she had no doubt that this was his intention. She was reluctant to descend, suddenly aware that this way of life was not for her. She had dabbled a toe in turbulent waters and found it wasn't to her liking.

She didn't want to enter the grotto, but Maxwell was there when she reached the bottom of the steps, holding out a hand towards her, his lean fingers strong as he drew her towards him.

'This will be a night you'll always remember,' he promised, then released her to welcome the others.

The grotto was lit by flambeau in brackets on the walls and heated by braziers. The seductive beat of tango music drifted from the sound equipment. It was bigger than

Freya remembered and his guests seemed enchanted with it. A bar had been set up and waiters carried round trays of snacks. She wondered where Maxwell had obtained these strapping young me. They were wearing next to nothing, their tanned torsos on display, and they seemed happy to accept caresses from either sex. They wore the briefest of leather short, and had gold chains attached to collars, with links that crossed their pectorals and waists, disappearing into their genital area.

Lola was in her element, her voluptuous body displayed through a semi-transparent Empire gown. She was flirting with everyone, male or female. At first it was a sedate gathering, with people talking and behaving sensibly, but as the wine went down and they relaxed, so they took advantage of whatever Maxwell had on offer. The grotto could have been designed for the purpose of sexual deviation. Not only was there a cross-piece, but benches where submissives could be tethered, flat on their backs or fronts, helpless to do other but become the willing victims of those who wished to flog and possess them. Racks carried whips, canes and paddles, and these were being employed without restraint. The air rang with cries and groans and the sounds of fornication.

It was becoming more abandoned. Above the din, Maxwell shouted, 'I need a virgin, but have been unable to find one.'

A bevy of scantily clad young women gathered around him. 'I'm very nearly a virgin,' cried one blond beauty. 'I've only had two lovers.'

'Take me and pretend,' said another, baring her breasts and snuggling up to him.

'If I have to pretend, then I'll choose my own for the ceremony,' he said, caressing each in turn. He looked straight at Freya who was trying to hide.' What about you, Miss Mullin? Will you play the game with me?'

She looked round wildly, seeking Moira, but she was embracing Giovanni, letting everyone know that he was out of bounds. 'I can't,' she answered, terrified that she would yield to this odd request.

'Can't? No one says that to me.' He thundered, glaring down at her. He gestured to a pair of men who were attired as semi-nude guards and, before she could move, had them seize her and carry her towards the whipping post.

The crowd parted to let them through, pausing in the midst of their own devious activities, catching on to what was about to take place. Freya struggled, kicked and shouted but to no avail. Within seconds she was chained to the post, wrists manacled, legs kept apart by a spreader. Maxwell approached her, touched her between the thighs, then addressed his guests.

'It was a tradition that Lord Sebastian, the onetime owner of this place, took a virgin once a year and offered up her maidenhood to the god Pan. I wanted to carry this on, but unfortunately it's nearly impossible to find one these days. So, we will pretend and, later, I'll show you the hidden shrine that no one but myself and close colleagues have seen yet. Meanwhile, I shall ravish this unwilling victim.'

The crowd cheered and surged close. Maxwell gripped the neck of Freya's dress and ripped it from her. Then he exposed his phallus and the cheers became louder, encouraging him.

'Maxwell, stop. Why are you humiliating me?' She hissed.

'You love it.' His arrogance knew no bounds and she

214

hated him for it. There was nothing for it. She couldn't fight him, her restraints were too strong, so she closed her eyes and waited for the pain and discomfort as he forced himself into her. It never came.

'Let her go,' a male voice demanded and she lifted her lids to see Grant elbowing his way through the spectators.

'What the hell…?' Maxwell turned to face him.

'You heard. Release her!'

Both men were glaring at each other and her. 'Is this what you want, Freya?' Maxwell shouted.

'Yes.' She didn't hesitate for a second. 'I don't like being put on show for your perverted friends.'

'You do realise that this will be the end of our friendship?' He seemed disconcerted for once, this usually confident man reduced.

'Friendship? Is that what it was? I don't think so, Max. You wanted to own me, and I wasn't having any. Now let me go. Find some other gullible woman who will be taken in by you.'

He signalled to his henchmen and she was unchained. Grant as there to catch her as she almost fell from the cross-piece. The crowd booed, robbed of their entertainment. Maxwell held up a hand for silence, saying, 'Don't worry, friends. I'll soon find someone else.' He looked at Freya and Grant and added, 'Get out!'

Moira was at her side, picking up the shawl and wrapping it round her. 'We'll come with you. He's just too much, bloody great show-off! Let's find our clothes and get out of here. Nice one, Grant.'

Everything had become clear to Freya when she heard Grant demanding her freedom. Maxwell was challenging, exciting, but she needed more than that. As they went to the changing-room, he drew her aside and said, 'Look

215

here. We can make a go of it. I think I've always loved you, that's why I could never find a girl who came anywhere close to how I remembered you.'

It was as if scales had been removed from her eyes and Freya saw him for what he was. A kind, generous, loving man who was sexually arousing and could be rough if she needed it. Why had she wasted time hankering after someone like Maxwell, difficult, selfish and utterly impossible?

'I shan't give up my house,' she said, leaning her head against his chest.

'I'm not asking you to, and I know you'll go on working. So shall I, wherever it takes me, but maybe you'll come too. Meanwhile, can we go back to your place and have sex?'

She laughed, feeling as if a great weight had been lifted from her shoulders. 'Try and stop me,' she said, and in his eyes she read the world and everything it had to offer.

Epilogue

Maxwell was too proud to accept defeat, but he let Freya go—for the time being. Gathering his flock around him, he proclaimed, 'I'm about to let you into a secret. Not only are you here, in the grotto, but there's something of far greater significance. Come with me.'

'Oh, we'll come!' chorused the scantily clad young women who had offered to be virgins.

He looked them over sardonically. He knew their type and was bored by them. Freya had the potential for more than a quick fuck. He had tried this and found that he wanted to take it further, whilst she, stubbornly independent, had refused him and gone off with his surveyor. It was more than just annoying.

He led the way to the shrine, and just for a moment, the crowd were silenced, staring in awe at the statue of Pan, the other gods, the gifts from ancient times. Jeff Plover strutted, pleased to let them know that he was already party to this.

'Will you tell British Heritage now?' He asked Maxwell.

'I shall make an announcement shortly. Of course, it will mean publicity, and I shall be asked to talk about it to the media and probably be commissioned to write a book. Lord Sebastian discovered it and left his journal and notes. It was he who used to bring maidens to the grotto and, after he had taken them, would present proof of their virginity as an offering to Pan. But as there is no one available tonight, I suggest you pay tribute to him by your own carnal activities. Do it in here, in front of him.'

They needed no second bidding, pagans at heart,

and soon the shrine echoed with their noisy copulating. There were men with men, women with women, as well as heterosexuals. Whips slashed bare flesh, white leather paddles landed on tender backsides. Some were manacled, others trussed to rings in the walls, and every orifice was used.

Lola sidled up to Maxwell, pushing aside the women who were offering themselves to him. 'Take me,' she urged. 'Close your eyes and pretend I've never been screwed. You know that I'd do anything for you.'

The adoration in her eyes was balm to his wounded pride. Here was someone he could trust, who truly loved him. Part of him despised her for it, and there was no fun in possessing such a woman, when he had promised himself that, if not a virgin, then it should be Freya. He snatched up a flogger and spun her round.

'On your knees, slut,' he commanded, standing in front of Pan, and raising the implement of punishment.

She obeyed, backside towards him and the flogger swooped down, the impact resounding above the grunts, shouts and screams of the rest. She was jerked forward with the force of the blow. He struck her again and again until she collapsed on the mosaic tiles. Then he hauled her up by her hair and took a position behind her, his phallus exposed for a moment before he drove it into her, ignoring her vagina but entering her arse.

She squealed and moaned, his hand beneath her, stimulating her clitoris. The noises made by his followers were music to his ears, adding to his arousal, and he came violently, resting against her for a moment, and then rising, removing the condom and laying it before Pan as his tribute to the god. He urged the others to do them same. If not virgin blood, then

218

Pan should have spunk as an offering.

This was only the beginning. He would have other women before the night was out, and his confidence returned. Freya and he were not over, not by a long chalk. She might prefer Grant for a while, but she would still be working at Daubeney Manor for some time yet, and there would be plenty of opportunity for them to meet. He smiled cynically. He'd even play the piano for her if this would make her change her mind.

The Darkest Master
Rhea Silva

Fleeing a failed relationship, Kirsty buys a business and a cottage in Cornwall. But set up in the hills behind the cottage is a strange house and in it lives the reclusive Dirk Stratten; rich and remote, but devastatingly attractive.

And with him comes his friend Lucian – equally as handsome yet infinitely more dangerous.

Gradually Kirsty gets drawn into their world and learns a truth stranger than any fiction. And beneath the cruelty and depravity lies a bargain that must be struck to save a life.

Rhea Silva once again weaves her spells and produces a seductive read that is atmospheric and bewitchingly erotic from the start.

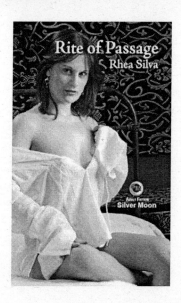

Rite of Passage
Rhea Silva

Adult Fiction
Silver Moon

Lady Verity Mandeville has just attained the age of majority and her father, the autocratic Earl of Tremadock has an unpleasant surprise for her; she has been betrothed to the ruler of a remote Eastern European country. Just as she is beginning to taste all the delights that Restoration England can offer, she is to be whisked off to marry Duke Marec.

What she finds when she arrives in Crocovia far exceeds any excess she could have imagined, for Marec is cruel and dominating; ruling his people with a rod of iron and taking his pleasure with any girl he chooses.

But slowly Verity comes to realise that the forests around Marec's castle hold a dark secret. But she must bring it into the light in time to save herself from falling under the spell of Marec's dominance, for she finds a strange pleasure in submitting to his every cruel whim.

Taming Maria
Rhea Silva

Young Lady Maria Granger stands ready to enter the
social scene of Georgian England.

As an orphan, she is the ward of the enigmatic Viscount
Strafford whom she has never met. But once she enters
into the tumultuous life of Regency London under the
tutelage of her mother's scandalously debauched sister,
Maria's good looks and fiery temperament thrust her into
the limelight.

Then her guardian appears and her life is never the
same again. Suddenly she is subject to discipline and
domination and although she tries to fight back, she finds
part of her welcomes his arrogance and cruelty.

Just as she is grappling with the problems of having
two lovers, she learns that her guardian may be a much
worse villain than even she believes.

Rhea Silva provides a rip-roaring tale of crime, passion
and debauchery set against the glittering backdrop of an
elegant but decadent epoch.

Atlanta is freshly back from college and staying with her uninhibited Aunt Jessica. And it is in her aunt's house that Atlanta's education really takes off. Accidentally she finds that when her aunt brings a lover home, there is a vantage point from which she can watch what happens. At first she is content just to be a voyeur but as what she sees becomes more and more outrageous, she is inevitably drawn into joining in.

From there it is a short step to being taken to a club to witness strange, ritual punishments. But whatever she witnesses and experiences, it only seems to drive her to want to experience more. Eagerly she dives into a whole new world of pleasure and pain; earning the delights of suffering.

And finally she comes to realise that her education can only be complete when the strict Sir Grenville is pleased with her… …but he is not easily pleased!

There are over 100 stunningly erotic novels of domination and submission in the Silver Moon catalogue. You can see the full range, including Club and Illustrated editions by writing to:

Convecto Reader Services
Box 101
City Business Centre
Station Rise
York
YO1 6HT

You will receive a copy of the latest issue of the Readers' Club magazine, with articles, features, reviews, adverts and news plus a full list of our publications and an order form.